# UNEXPECTED GIFTS

## A CASTLE MOUNTAIN LODGE ROMANCE

### ELENA AITKEN

INK BLOT COMMUNICATIONS

# ALSO BY ELENA AITKEN

Only for a Moment

One more Moment

In this Moment

From this Moment

Our Perfect Moment

**The Springs Series**

Summer of Change

Falling Into Forever

Second Glances (Novella)

Winter's Burn

Midnight Springs

She's Making A List (Holiday Novella)

Fighting For Forever (Novella)

Summit of Desire

Summit of Seduction

Summit of Passion

The Springs Collection: Volume 1

The Springs Collection: Volume 2

The Springs Collection: Volume 3

The Springs Complete Collection - Books 1-10

**Destination Paradise**

Shelter by the Sea

Escape to the Sun

Hidden in the Sand - Available Soon!

**Bears of Grizzly Ridge**

His to Protect

His to Seduce

His to Claim

Hers to Take

His to Defend

His to Tame

His to Seek

Hers for the Season

Bears of Grizzly Ridge: Books 1-4

Bears of Grizzly Ridge: Books 5-8

**Escape Collection**

Nothing Stays in Vegas

Return to Vegas

Drawing Free

Sugar Crash

Composing Myself

Betty & Veronica

The Escape Collection

**Halfway Series**

Halfway to Nowhere

Halfway in Between

Halfway to Christmas

# UNEXPECTED GIFTS

*Snowed in for Christmas...She only wants to ignore it. But he's determined to show her everything the season has to offer...including love.*

# 1

DECEMBER 21

*U*nable to take one more second, Andi Williams spun around and hit the power button on the stereo. Bing Crosby's Winter Wonderland cut off mid-wonder and blissful silence filled the space.

Her best friend and business partner, Eva, appeared from the storage room wearing antlers and holding two hats: a Santa in one hand, an elf in the other. She glanced at the mute stereo and shot Andi a look. "Which do you think?" she asked and held up the hats.

"Go with the reindeer," she said. "Santa is overdone and if you dress as an elf, people might get the wrong idea about Santa's little helper." With Eva's tall, curvy body, pretty much anything she wore gave men the wrong idea.

"It's a party for the Senior Mens' curling team." Eva tossed the other two hats behind her onto a shelf and moved over to the stereo, flicking it on again.

Party Hearty, their event planning business, was stuffed into a tiny office, with barely enough room for their desks and a couch for client meetings. Despite the small space, Eva felt it was crucial to maintain a festive atmosphere for potential clients, which, in her opinion, meant carols on repeat play and the overpowering scent of cinnamon and apple spice. For Andi, it was less festive and more like torture to be constantly surrounded by a reminder of the holidays.

"Definitely the reindeer then," Andi said, trying her best to ignore the music. "When did we get the curling team? I don't remember it in the books."

Andi was in charge of bookings and most of the business side for Party Hearty, but this year, the holiday season had been their busiest ever. She'd be relieved when it was over. It's not that Andi was dreading the holiday season because it meant working late into the night, or juggling schedules, or even trying to find enough staff to work each party; no, it was because Christmas this year represented everything Andi was supposed to have, and didn't.

"It was a last-minute thing," Eva said. "They called yesterday and the party's this Saturday. Short notice, means lots of extra cash. Plus, it's a no-brainer. I already have the girls working out the details."

The 'girls' were the two college students Andi had hired at the beginning of November. They'd been a blessing and naturals at the party business, as college students usually were. Regardless, their presence meant Andi could stay in the office and as far away from the actual parties as possible. Exactly where she wanted to be.

"What's in the bags?" Eva asked and pointed to the pile of packages stacked next to Andi's desk. "Don't tell me you have presents in there? I thought you hated Christmas?"

Andi sighed and rolled her eyes. "It's not that I hate Christmas..."

"Whatever you say."

"I got the boys their gifts," Andi said. "Watching my little brothers open their presents is going to be the only saving grace to this stupid holiday." She flopped backwards, sinking into her leather chair. Her desk was organized into neat piles of invoices, to-do lists, and a growing stack of unopened Christmas cards and invitations. Andi moved a magazine so it was covering the envelopes. "Three is the perfect age for this stuff. And when they see the drums I got them, they're going to go crazy." Andi flashed a wicked smile.

"Your dad is going to kill you," Eva said.

"It's his own fault for having twins at his age. Besides, isn't that my job as the older half-sister?"

Eva didn't answer her. Instead, she tossed a thick, red envelope on her desk. "This came for you today."

Andi knew what it was before she even turned it over to read the calligraphy on the front. The invitation to the Porter's Annual Night Before, The Night Before, Christmas Party. Her stomach churned and for a brief, terrifying moment she thought she might throw up on her desk, right on top of the offending envelope in all its glossy, card stock weighted glory.

Why did they send her an invitation this year? They had to know she wouldn't go. How could she show her face in a room filled with her ex's family and friends? Why would she want to?

"Damn, I should have recycled it," Eva said. She appeared in front of Andi, her face creased with concern. "I'm sorry. I knew I shouldn't have given it to you. Do you need a drink? I can get you a bottle of water. I think we might even have some wine in the back. I can get you what—"

"I'm fine." Andi took a deep breath and sat up straight. The only way to make it was to fake it, so she slapped both hands on her desk and stood. "Now," she said. "What needs to be done?"

Eva stared at Andi as if she'd spontaneously grown a horn out of her forehead.

"What?" Andi asked. "We have parties to plan, don't we? After all, that is what people pay us to do, right?" She walked as she spoke, moving to the wall where they kept clipboards for each event.

"Andi, it's okay."

"What's okay?" She flipped through the pages, not seeing any of the lists.

"Sit." Eva pushed a chair towards her.

"I'm fine."

"Sit," she said again. This time there was enough force behind her voice that Andi stopped and looked at her friend. "It's okay," she said softly.

"I can't do this," Andi whispered. She could feel the tears building in the corners of her eyes and she hated herself for them. She'd promised herself months ago that she wouldn't cry. Tears didn't do any good. They never had. "I don't think I can do this."

"You don't have to go to the party."

"No," she said and waved her arms around the room. "I can't do this. Any of this. Christmas. The holidays. The happy, cheerful people. The kids singing carols and eating candy. Santa. Gingerbread. Any of it. Christmas is for families."

"You have a family," Eva said gently.

"You know what I mean." Andi grabbed a tissue and dabbed her eyes before the tears could leak out.

"I know," Eva said. She pulled a chair next to her friend and held her hand tight. "Andi, you will have a family. It wasn't—"

"Don't you dare say it wasn't meant to be." She snatched her hand away. For the last eight months—since her daughter had been stillborn—Andi had heard those words too much. They were what people said when they didn't know what else to say. They were the words uttered by those who couldn't handle seeing her in pain and thought she should just get over it. How did you get over losing a baby? How could you ever get over pain like that?

"I wasn't going to say that," Eva said. "I was going to say... okay, I was going to say that. But only because Blaine wasn't right for you, not because of anything else. He's a total jerk and he should've stood by you. What kind of guy takes off after something like that? I mean—"

"Please." Andi held her hand up to stop her friend's tirade. Eva had never liked Blaine. From the moment they'd been introduced, she'd declared him a pretty boy who was too into himself and his career. She never understood what Andi saw in him. She didn't see the tender side of Blaine that Andi did. The way they used to talk for hours about the future, how he used to encourage Andi to make Party Hearty bigger, to expand and become the biggest party planning firm in Calgary. And when Andi was pregnant with their child, how he'd sit for hours with his hand on her belly, talking to the baby and poring through name books with her. They'd talked about getting married after finding out they were expecting, and there wasn't a doubt in Andi's mind that it would be perfect. Until it wasn't.

"Can we talk about something else?" Andi said. "Are you sure you don't need me for any of the parties next week?"

Eva scooted her chair back to her own desk and grabbed her planner. "You know I don't," she said. "They're all taken care of. We have that charity ball on the twenty-third and then the Anderson gig on Boxing Day. I have the girls lined up. We're good to go."

"Really, Eva, I don't mind being there if you need me."

"I don't need you," she said with a grin. "Besides, you'd be miserable acting like you were full of festive joy. No offense, but you're not really very good at pretending."

"None taken," she mumbled.

"You know, if you really don't want to be around, we got a promo invite from the Castle Mountain Lodge for a villa. You can use it."

The Castle Mountain Lodge was only two hours from the city, but it might as well have been a world away. Nestled in the mountains, the Lodge had a reputation as a mountain hideaway far away from the rest of the world. It would be the perfect place to escape to. The thought of hiding away in the forest, reading a good book in front of a crackling fire until the holidays were over, did have its appeal.

"For when?" Andi asked.

"It's actually good through to the twenty-sixth. You can hide from the whole holiday." Eva dug in a pile on her desk. Producing the invitation, she tossed it to Andi. "But I thought you were spending Christmas with your dad? Didn't you say, and I quote, 'watching my little brothers open their presents is going to be the only saving grace to this stupid holiday'?"

Andi smiled at the thought of her twin brothers. They were busy, full of mischief and fun, but best of all they adored their half-sister, which made their mother, who was only three years older than Andi herself, miserable. She'd give up the dream of hiding at the Lodge, but only for them.

"It's true," she said. "I'll tolerate Roxanne and her awful cooking to see the boys. Maybe I can pretend that we're all one big happy family and it won't be so bad."

Eva smiled, but before she could say anything, the phone rang. Eva answered with a jingle in her voice, "Good afternoon. It's a happy holiday season at Party Hearty."

Andi rolled her eyes and turned back to the piles on her desk.

"Yes, Mr. Williams, she's right here. Let me put you through."

Eva pressed the button to put him on hold and said, "Speak of the devil. He's on line one. I'll be in the storage room if you need me. I think I'm going to need some mistletoe for the curlers."

Andi laughed along with her and was still laughing when she picked up the phone. "Hi, Dad."

"Hi, sugar. How's work today? Are you girls busy over there?"

Leave it to Dad to put business first.

"Very," she said. "'Tis the season and all that. What's up?"

There was a silence on the line and in that instant, Andi knew she wasn't going to like what she heard.

"Well," he said after a moment. "I'm afraid I don't have very good news. I know you were looking forward to a family Christmas this year."

'Looking forward to', weren't really the words she would have chosen. More like '"would tolerate"'.

"But plans have changed," Andi's dad was still talking.

"What do you mean, plans have changed? Christmas is in five days."

"That's just it. Roxanne decided she'd like to go to Disney World this year and the boys are at a good age for the Magic Kingdom and she found a great last-minute deal and—"

"Wait," Andi stopped him. "Did I hear you right? You're ditching me, your only daughter, to spend the holidays with Mickey Mouse?" Andi's chest tightened and she took a sip of water.

"We leave tonight."

"I've never been to Disney."

"Did you want to come?"

"You know I don't."

"We'll be back for New Year's, if you want to come over then?"

The only thing more pathetic than the prospect of spending Christmas alone, was the idea of spending New Year's Eve with her father and his child bride.

"No thanks," she said.

"What about your mother?"

"She's on a cruise with Val," Andi said. "I told you that." And she had, but he'd likely blocked it from his memory, as he did with any reminder that his first wife had left him for another woman.

"Well, you're always saying how busy you are at this time of the year and—"

"Don't worry, Dad. I'll be fine," she muttered. "Merry Christmas."

She hung up before he could return her well wishes. She didn't want to hear them.

"Eva," she called in to the back room. "Where did you put that promo invite for Castle Mountain Lodge?"

# 2

DECEMBER 22

*C*olin Hartford steered his four-wheel drive up the windy road leading to the Castle Mountain Lodge. His tires crunched on the freshly fallen snow. The plows couldn't keep up with the thick white stuff covering the roads and Colin was pretty sure they'd given up on trying to keep the roads clear. He hadn't seen one in over an hour. The weather forecast had said it would be a white Christmas, but they hadn't said anything about a blizzard. It took all his concentration to navigate the icy roads. Combined with the low visibility, the dense pines on both sides of the road gave him the sense that he was driving farther and farther into the middle of nowhere. But Rose, his grandmotherly assistant, had assured him that the Lodge had full resort facilities. Plus, Rose had promised it was famous for the grand holiday festivities it put on. It was perfect for his first Christmas back in Canada.

He'd had enough of beaches and hot sun to ring in the holidays. Colin craved some old-fashioned carols, ice skating, gingerbread houses and lots of snow. Five years away was enough to make him miss the cold weather. It didn't matter what anyone said; Christmas without snow was just wrong.

After a few minutes of steady climbing up the steep mountain road, the trees began to thin, and soon they were covered in white and red lights, illuminating the drive as the sun began to set. Like a candy cane lane, Colin thought with excitement. He couldn't keep the grin off his face but he fought the urge to accelerate. He couldn't wait to start experiencing everything the season had to offer, but he didn't think digging the Jeep out of a snow drift was a good way to start.

Even driving slowly, it didn't take long before buildings and cabins came into view. They were all joined by interconnected pathways, loosely arranged around a large pond and common area. The main lodge served as the focus of the tiny village, placed at the far end of the pond. The Lodge was impressive. Certainly a lot nicer than the hotels Colin had been living out of in the Caribbean for the last few years.

He pulled up to the main entrance, where a valet opened his door.

"Good evening, sir," the valet said. "Welcome to Castle Mountain Lodge."

"Thank you." Colin unfolded his large frame from the vehicle and grabbed his bag out of the back. A bellboy appeared, but Colin waved him away. "This is it, really," he said, gesturing to his duffle.

"Carmen at the desk will get you settled, and I'll take care of your car. Enjoy your stay, sir. And Merry Christmas."

Colin smiled. It would be a merry Christmas. He looked around through the falling snow at the trees and took a deep breath of mountain air. How could it not be when this beauty surrounded him?

The main doors opened up to a majestic three-story room. Exposed timbers framed the walls and vaulted ceiling. Colin moved through the lobby, taking in the rustic holiday atmosphere. There were fresh pine boughs draped around the banisters leading to the upper stories and a smell of spice and cinnamon filled the air. Before heading to the check-in desk, he stopped to admire a massive tree decorated with oversized white pine cones, holly berries, and strands of popcorn that stood in the center of the lobby. A fire crackled in the large river rock hearth across the room and a piano player filled the space with the soft sounds of carols.

Colin stood for a moment taking it all in. It was just as Rose promised. A scene right out of a movie, or one of those home and style magazines she was always reading. Eager to get checked in and start participating in some festive activities, he found the front desk and spotted a woman standing behind it with Carmen on her name tag. She was madly typing something into her computer and repeatedly running her hands through her hair. As Colin got closer, he could hear her apologizing to a petite dark-haired woman in front of him at the desk.

"I'm so sorry, Ms Williams," Carmen said. "I wish there was more that I could do."

"But you sent us the invitation," the woman said. "How can you not have a room for me, when you sent it?"

There was something about her voice that was familiar. But that was impossible. He barely knew anyone in Canada anymore; he'd been gone so long.

"I'm so sorry," Carmen said again. "We did have the room but the invitation was sent a few weeks ago and we expected that since we didn't hear from you or your company, you would be declining the offer. I can offer you and your company another complimentary stay as well as some dinner vouchers for the restaurant."

The woman, her back still to Colin, shook her head. "Is there anywhere else nearby?"

"There's a bed and breakfast about twenty miles down the mountain. I could call them to see if they have a room?"

It was a blizzard out there. If the highways weren't already closed, they would be soon. Colin was about to say so, but Carmen was still talking.

"We usually keep a few extra rooms open," Carmen said, as she reached for the phone, "just in case of a situation like this, but with the holiday season upon us...well, we did have one villa available, but it was booked last minute. Just yesterday in fact."

Rose had made his reservation only yesterday, Colin thought. She hadn't told him she'd secured him a villa. He made a mental note to talk to her about excessive spending.

"What am I supposed to do now?" the woman said.

"Ms Williams, I can't tell you how sorry we are about the mix-up. Let me make the call for you."

The woman waved her hand. "No, it's fine," she said, and turned around so quickly, she almost smacked right into Colin's chest and for the first time, he saw her face. She was stunning. And very familiar. It wasn't just her voice. He knew this woman. She swiped her black hair away from her eyes with a quick, angry wipe. Her dark eyes contrasted sharply against her pale skin, and if he hadn't been eavesdropping, Colin might have missed the unshed tears that glistened in the corners.

"Do I know you?" he asked, before she could move past him.

The woman stopped short and looked up at him. He watched as a flash of recognition crossed her face, but then her eyes narrowed and she said, "No. I don't think so."

Colin stared at her for a moment. He was sure he knew her. Someone from high school maybe?

"Did you go to Mountain View High?" he asked.

"No," she said and turned away again. While he watched, she pulled her hair off her face into a ponytail. When she turned back, Colin's memory clicked into place.

Blaine Porter's girlfriend. He'd known Blaine since grade school, and even though they'd ended up more as rivals than friends over the years, they occasionally ran into each other. When Blaine had called to tell Colin he was visiting St. Lucia with his girlfriend last year, Colin had hooked up with the couple for dinner and drinks. It had only been one evening, and it was awhile ago, but there was no doubt that's why she looked so familiar.

"Wait," Colin said. "I do know you."

The look that crossed over her face left no room for doubt that she knew him too.

"Blaine's girlfriend," he said. "St. Lucia. Remember?"

"I remember."

Colin looked around the room. "It's Andi, right? Is Blaine here with you? I haven't—"

The look on her face stopped him.

"He's not here," she said. Her voice was soft, but hard. Evidently it had been too long since he'd caught up with Blaine.

"The two of you aren't together anymore?"

Her silence and the hard look in her eyes was the only answer he needed.

"I should get going before it gets too late." Andi turned and moved to leave but before she could get away, Colin reached out and grabbed her arm.

"Wait," he said. "You can't go out in that."

She turned to look out the picture windows, where the outside lights illuminated the increasing snowdrifts, and the snow still fell from the sky.

"What am I going to do now?" She didn't speak to Colin directly, but he could tell she was near tears.

"Excuse me," Colin said, turning to Carmen. "How big are these villas?"

"I'm sorry, sir?"

"The villas," he said, and glanced back at the woman who

was watching the exchange. "I believe my assistant booked me a villa yesterday, and I really don't need that much space."

Carmen straightened behind the desk and clicked some keys on her computer. "What was your name, Sir?"

"Hartford. Colin Hartford," he said, his eyes still on the woman next to him. She didn't say anything.

"Yes," Carmen said. "You are registered in a villa. They're really quite large. Twelve hundred square feet. Three bedrooms, two bathrooms, and a small kitchen."

Colin turned to Andi who still hadn't said anything. "I know this seems strange, but we do kind of know each other and you really have no place to stay. Would you consider taking a room? It's snowing really hard out there, and I can't in good conscience let you drive back down the mountain tonight."

She opened her mouth to speak, but before she could, Carmen interrupted. "That's a very generous offer, Mr. Hartford, but—"

"Let her answer," he said and turned back to Andi.

She cleared her throat and said, "I don't know. I—"

"I would suggest that you call Blaine for a character reference," he said. "But something tells me that wouldn't work in my favor and I honestly can't be sure he'd give me a glowing report either. So what about the fact that I haven't seen or spoken to him in over a year? Does that help?"

Andi smiled again. "Actually, it does."

"See? I really am a good guy. Even if I didn't choose my childhood friends very well."

That made her smile again but before she could say anything, the main doors opened and the doorman rushed into the lobby in a blast of snow and icy air. "It's nasty out there," he said. "You folks are lucky you got here when you did. We just heard over the radio that the highway has been closed." He rubbed his hands together and blew on them to warm up.

Andi looked past the doorman, out to the building blizzard outside. With a sigh, she turned to Colin, and said, "Well, being friends with Blaine is certainly not a ringing endorsement, but it doesn't look like I have a lot of options."

"Ms Williams," Carmen said, "we could offer you a couch in the lobby, or maybe even in the staff quarters."

Both Colin and Andi turned to stare at Carmen.

"Or," Colin said slowly, "you can take one of my extra rooms. I swear, I'm perfectly normal. And it has to be more comfortable than a couch somewhere."

"I'll admit, an extra room sounds a lot better than sleeping on a couch," Andi said to Carmen before turning to Colin. "And from what I remember about you in St. Lucia, you're fairly normal. Even though I'm not sure ordering flying fish off the menu is all that normal."

"You remember?"

She shrugged.

"So, I'll take that as a yes?" Colin asked. "And I promise, I'm not a crazy ax murderer or anything." He swung his duffle around so she could see it. "See? An ax wouldn't fit."

Andi glanced at the bag and gave Colin a pointed look. "Like I said, I don't seem to have much of a choice. But if I'm going to spend time with any of Blaine's friends, I'm going to need a drink."

"We're not—"

"I know, I know." She held up her hand. "You're not besties. I got it."

"We'll take care of your bags, Ms Williams," Carmen said, and before Colin could say anything, Andi started walking to the bar situated at the other end of the lobby.

In a hurry to join her, he quickly finished the check-in process and left his own bag to be delivered to his room. Colin couldn't remember much about their brief dinner meeting in St.

Lucia, only that Blaine had phoned him out of the blue to let him know that they were visiting the island. The entire visit seemed more like a reason for Blaine to show off his beautiful fiancée and brag to Colin about his successful business than anything else. But Blaine had always been that way. Even as kids, he used every chance he got to show off or brag about what he had and what he could do.

Colin's first impression of Andi that night had been that she was beautiful and smart, but he couldn't for the life of him figure out why she was with Blaine. Not that Blaine was all bad; they'd hung out in the same circle, and at one time, they'd been close friends. But things change, and certainly after high school there hadn't been much of a friendship between them, unless you could call Blaine's constant one-upmanship a friendship. But there'd been something about Blaine and Andi together that didn't sit right with Colin then. And now as he crossed the lobby towards the bar, Colin couldn't help but smile at the thought that Blaine would hate the fact that he was about to spend time with his ex. His very beautiful ex.

*A*ndi twisted her napkin in her hand and looked up to where Colin was waiting for drinks at the bar. What was she thinking, staying in a strange man's hotel room in the middle of the mountains? But that was the problem, wasn't it? He wasn't really a stranger. Andi sighed and rubbed her temples. She'd recognized him right away and had hoped he wouldn't remember her. What were the odds that she'd run into someone who knew Blaine? Especially when she was trying to flee anything that reminded her of him? This really wasn't her week.

Andi smiled, thinking of how shocked Eva would be to find out about her accommodations. She'd probably think it was a great idea for Andi to bust out of her typical groove. It's not like she had a lot of choices, though, she told herself again. Besides, Colin had seemed normal enough when they'd met that one time in St. Lucia, and from what she could remember, Colin had been very friendly and not at all like Blaine's usual stuck-up friends. He'd tried, without much success, to include her in the conversation but Blaine had seemed bent on telling Colin about his latest business acquisitions and how well he was doing. Andi remembered the fight they'd had later that night when she accused Blaine of behaving like a jerk. He didn't get like that often, but every once in a while...

Andi's thoughts drifted off when Colin turned from the bar holding a glass of wine and a bottle of beer. Colin looked like the total opposite of Blaine, which maybe had something to do with the animosity between them. Where Blaine was always well-groomed, wearing a shirt and tie, this man wore faded jeans and a worn t-shirt that hugged his chest. Overdue for a haircut, his shaggy hair persistently fell over one eye in a way Andi would normally find annoying. But there was something about the way Colin brushed it off his face that Andi found ridiculously sexy. In fact, he did seem to have the most unnerving way of making her stomach flutter every time he looked at her.

"I hope Shiraz is okay?" he asked, as he reached the table and put the glass in front of her. "You didn't tell me your preference, so I guessed."

"Shiraz is great." She took a sip of her drink in an effort to squash the sudden and completely ridiculous urge to reach out and touch the scruff on his chin. What was wrong with her?

Colin reclined in the chair across from her and took a long pull on his beer. When he put the bottle down, his green eyes locked on hers and they looked so familiar that for a moment, Andi forgot that she barely knew anything about him.

"So, Andi," he said, and a smile tugged at the corner of his lips. "It just occurred to me that I offered you a room in my villa and all I really know about you is that you like red wine, you don't plan ahead by confirming reservations, and you get a really sour look on your face when I mention Blaine."

She opened her mouth to object, but before she did, closed it again. There was nothing to protest. She really didn't like the mention of Blaine's name and even though it wasn't her fault that the reservation wasn't confirmed, it didn't really matter. Of course, she should have known that Eva wouldn't have checked. There was a reason Andi took care of the business side of Party Hearty.

Andi took another sip of her wine. She swirled it around in her mouth before swallowing and responding. "What do you want to know?"

"Well, I'm assuming that you don't want to talk about Blaine."

"You assume correctly."

"Right. And since my relationship with him seems to depend solely on him telling me how great he is every few years, why don't we just pretend that we don't have that in common? That way you can't hold it against me."

Andi raised her glass. There was something endearing about him and his effort to make her feel more comfortable. "Deal," she said.

They clinked glasses, and after taking a drink, Colin said, "I've already assured you that I'm not an ax murderer. How about a similar assurance?"

"I've been rehabilitated," she said with a straight face.

"Good thing." Colin laughed. "I suppose I should have asked if you had an ax in your bag."

She raised her eyebrows and laughed along with him.

"Now that we have the important details cleared up," he said after a moment, "there's something I have to know. Is Andi your full name or is it short for something?"

Andi took another sip of her wine and fiddled with the napkin. "Really? That's what you *have* to know?"

"What? We're trying to get to know each other, aren't we?" he asked in mock defense. "It's a fair question."

She found herself smiling again, and answered, "You can call me Andi."

"You didn't answer my question," Colin said. "Is that what I should call you, or is that your actual name?"

"Believe it or not, it is my actual name," she said, and looked down at her napkin. "I wish I could say it was short for something, but really my dad was convinced I would be a boy and when I wasn't, he decided the next best thing to having a son would be to pretend I was one."

"Wow," he said. The light atmosphere between them shifted, and when she looked up, there was a look of concern on his face. "So I assume the two of you aren't close?"

Andi shrugged. "We were actually, but now he really does have those sons he wanted so bad, along with a new wife. So he's pretty busy with them."

"And your mom?"

Andi took another sip of her wine before answering. With any other guy, she would have balked at such intimate questions, but there was something about Colin and she couldn't remember the last time she felt so relaxed with a man. He was incredibly easy to talk to and he genuinely seemed interested. Heck, she'd even told him the story behind her name and she couldn't remember the last time she'd ever done that. With anyone.

"My mom and I are close."

"Then why are you here?" He asked the question gently. "Holidays are supposed to be for friends and family. Why are you here alone?"

"I could ask you the same thing."

"Touché." He picked up his beer bottle and raised it to her, diffusing the tension in the air.

They sat in silence for a few minutes. Andi pretended not to notice the way he studied her. She focused instead on the picture windows framing the winter wonderland scene outside. The snow was falling even heavier than when she'd arrived and was forming a thick blanket over the courtyard. It was beautiful, but it would also mean the drive back down the mountains to the city would be treacherous. She was used to winter driving, but winter driving in the unpredictable mountains was a different story.

"The highways are going to be a mess," Colin said, reading her mind. "I barely got here and I have four-wheel drive."

She nodded and raised her glass to her mouth.

"Don't worry about staying," he said. "I already promised you I'm a nice guy. And besides, it's not good to be alone on the holidays."

She flipped in her chair so she was staring at him head-on. "Who said I was going to be alone?"

"Who said I was talking about you?"

HE DIDN'T THINK she would agree to it. It was a spur-of-the-moment offer to share his villa with her, but she was stranded, and kind of an old friend, and besides, he was alone. Colin was determined to make this Christmas the best he'd had in years. With his recent history, it wasn't going to be hard to top the past, but having Andi around, even temporarily, would definitely make things more interesting.

Colin swiped the card in the key lock and held the door open for Andi.

"Thank you." She swept past him, her arm brushing his chest. "Sorry," she said, turning around to look at him. The slight touch—despite the barriers of thick coats—had sparked something, and he could tell by the look in her eyes that she'd felt it too.

He shrugged and Andi turned to enter the villa.

Colin assumed since she'd received a promo invitation from

her company, that she'd been on the receiving end of many such offers, and had probably seen her fair share of elegant accommodations. Even so, how could she not be impressed with the room? He had to make a dedicated effort to keep his own mouth from hanging open in shock as he entered behind her, followed by the bellboy with a trolley of her luggage.

A smaller scale of the lobby in the main building, this room was two stories of vaulted, wood beam ceilings. A fire had been laid in the rock work fireplace and there was even a Christmas tree, fully decorated, in the center of the window. With the snow still falling outside, the room looked like it belonged on a greeting card.

"What do you think?" he asked Andi. "Have you been here before?"

She turned to face him but he couldn't read the expression on her face.

"I've stayed at the Lodge before, but never in a villa. This is..." She stopped and spun slowly, encompassing the room with her arms. "Amazing," she finished. When she stopped moving, she stood in front of him, and he was rewarded with a smile on her face that made her eyes sparkle. He realized he hadn't seen such an honest smile from her yet. It was gorgeous. "I could do without all the decorations, though," she added.

"I must admit," he said. "I didn't expect anything like this either. But I like it." He watched for her reaction, and added, "And I think the Christmas decorations are a nice touch."

"Sir," the bellboy said, interrupting them. "Which room shall I put the bags in?"

Colin turned. He'd forgotten the bellboy was still there. "Oh." He glanced at Andi, who was now standing at the window, staring outside. "You can put them all in the master suite," he said to the boy, "except the duffle bag. Choose another room for that one."

The bellboy nodded and turned to carry out his duty, but not before Colin noticed the look on his face. No doubt the kid was likely thinking that if he had a woman as beautiful as Andi in his villa, there would not be separate rooms involved.

"Make yourself at home," Colin said to Andi. "I really don't want you to feel like a guest. Please just think of it as your space."

She turned away from the window at the sound of his voice. He couldn't be sure, but it looked like she was fighting back tears. "Thank you," she said. "I mean it, Colin. You didn't have to do this. But I really appreciate you letting me stay here. I don't think I could—"

"Will there be anything else, sir?" the bellboy asked, appearing at Colin's side. "Would you like me to show you the controls for the hot tub?"

"There's a hot tub?" he asked.

"Of course, sir. On the deck. It's quite simple to use."

"I'm sure it is," Colin said. "I think we'll be fine. Thank you."

He handed over a twenty-dollar bill and the boy disappeared.

Colin wanted to finish the conversation with Andi. He wanted to know more about why she was here, why she wasn't with Blaine, and just more about her, period. But when he turned his attention back to her, she was in the small kitchen, searching through the cupboards.

He watched her for a minute before asking, "Looking for something?"

She looked up and smiled. "Did you know they stocked the fridge? You have quite the spread here."

"You mean, *we* have. I told you, this is your place too."

A look crossed over her face. "You know," she said. "I just realized that I didn't get a chance to ask you about your situation. Won't your girlfriend be upset that I'm here?"

Colin crossed his arms. She was obviously fishing for information, and by the smirk on her pretty face, she already knew the answer to her question.

"I don't have a girlfriend," he said. "Women are nothing but trouble." Her smile faltered a little at his gruffness and he immediately softened his tone. "I prefer to be single. Besides, there isn't room for women in my life, at least not for anything long-term."

"Well, I guess that's good then," she said. "I wouldn't want some jealous woman chasing after me." Her smile was back, teasing him, sparking something inside him.

There was no way that Blaine's ex would be interested in a little festive fling. Would she? Colin pushed the thought from his mind. It didn't matter how attracted to her he was. Some things were off-limits.

"Are you hungry?" he said, and pointed to the jar of almonds she'd pulled out of the cupboard. "We could go find one of the restaurants, or if there's something to cook here...or, maybe you don't want to spend all your time with me. I'm sure you have something you want to be doing. After all, you didn't plan on spending your holidays with a stranger." As soon as the words came out of his mouth, he realized how much he hoped she didn't have any other plans. What was it about this woman? He'd never been so unsure of himself around the ladies.

Colin waited while Andi walked around the kitchen island, back into the living room. She looked like she wanted to say something, but instead, she stopped and said, "You know, you're right. I should probably get my things unpacked."

"Of course." He pointed her towards the room the bellboy had put her bags in and watched her go down the hall. As soon as she was out of sight, Colin wished she were back. It had been a very long time since a woman had stirred such intense feelings in him and intrigued him so completely. The last time had been a very long time ago.

And remember how well that turned out? he reminded himself. No, he wouldn't get involved. No matter how strong the pull towards her might be.

## 4

---

*I*t didn't take long for Andi to unpack her bags and get organized. It was kind of strange taking the master bedroom, but when she'd gone back into the living room to ask Colin about it, he was gone. It was stupid but she was disappointed that he wasn't there. She liked him. There was something about him that allowed her to relax and it was nice to spend time with a man without it feeling forced. She felt more comfortable around Colin, who was still a relative stranger, than with Blaine, at least at the end.

Eva would roll her eyes at that. She was always telling her that relationships shouldn't be so hard. At the thought of her friend, Andi had to laugh. She would never believe where Andi was staying. She grabbed her cell phone and walked to the window to call her.

The phone went straight to voicemail. Of course Eva would be busy putting the finishing touches on the events this week. Andi had a flash of guilt. She should be there to help out. After all, it was her company, too.

"Hi," she said into the phone. "It's me. I just wanted to tell you I got here alright and my reservation got messed up. But you'll never guess how it worked out." Andi smiled, knowing her message would drive her friend crazy with wonder. "Anyway, let me know how everything's going. We'll talk soon."

After she hung up the phone, she didn't know what to do with herself. She hadn't thought much beyond getting out of the city for the holidays. She'd wanted to hide, and the mountains seemed to be a good place to do it. But she hadn't considered what she might do once she arrived. A glance at the clock on the nightstand told her it was still a bit early for dinner, which was fine with her, she didn't want to be inside anyway.

The snow was still falling, but it didn't seem to be coming down quite so hard. She looked through the window at the darkening village and Andi watched the lights in the nearby buildings come on, giving the covered earth a sparkle. The scene outside, while frosty, also looked inviting. The Lodge staff were out, busy with shovels and mini snowplows, doing their best to clear the paths. They'd be clear enough to walk on. Andi grabbed her gloves, hat, and coat and headed out for a walk.

Right before she let the door of the villa close behind her, she wondered if she should leave Colin a note telling him where she'd gone. But he hadn't left her one. And why should he? He had told her to make herself at home, and he would have his own things to do.

Shoving thoughts of Colin out of her head, Andi tucked her hands into her pockets and strode out onto the cleared walkway. She'd noticed the path system when they made their way from the main lodge earlier and the bellboy had told them the trails were all well-lit and maintained. When she asked, he told her they traveled through the village, and made up a total of fifteen kilometers. The system was designed so there was no need to drive anywhere. Everything was in walking distance. With the chill in the air, Andi was pretty sure she would turn into an ice cube before she walked all fifteen kilometers, but she was definitely looking forward to stretching her legs for a little bit.

Letting the trails lead her away from the buildings, Andi walked where the trees started getting thicker. She wasn't the only one with the idea of an evening stroll and there were other guests out as well; couples holding hands, a few families, and every once in a while she saw another lone walker like herself.

Her thoughts drifted to Colin. What was his story? Why was such a handsome man alone for Christmas? There could be a million explanations and he had made it pretty clear that he didn't want anything to do with a relationship, but there had to be more to it than that. Blaine had only mentioned him the once, right before their trip to St. Lucia, and she got the distinct impression that although they'd hung out as kids, they weren't all that close. Their dinner had been more about proving to Colin how great Blaine had turned out than a chance to catch up with a friend. There had to be a story behind that. Maybe something happened between them in high school? Instead of creating stories in her head, Andi resolved to ask him about it when she saw him again. If she saw him again. She didn't know anything about the man or why he was alone during Christmas. Maybe he was at the Lodge for business, although she couldn't imagine what business he would have in the mountains the week of Christmas.

Distracted by her thoughts, she didn't notice the little boy until he crashed into her legs.

"Oh," she said, bending down to help him up. "Are you okay?"

The moment she spoke, the little boy burst into tears.

Andi glanced around, looking for a parent. She didn't know how to handle kids, especially ones who were crying. For the last eight months, she'd done her best to avoid children, even her half-brothers, when she could manage it.

She looked around desperately, but there was no one around except her and the little boy, whose cries had only become more intense. She crouched and took his hand. "It's okay," she said, trying her best to sound calm. She could feel her body shaking and hoped he wouldn't notice. "Where's your mom?"

The boy looked to be about four. "I'm lost," he managed to choke out between sobs.

"Don't worry," she said. "We'll go find your mommy, okay?"

The little boy nodded and wiped his nose with the back of his mittened hand. She took his hand in hers and stood. They only got a few steps when she heard a woman's voice calling through the trees. A moment later, the woman turned the corner on the path and spotted them.

"Noah," she called and jogged—as best she could with a baby strapped to her chest—towards them.

The little boy dropped Andi's hand and ran towards his mom. Andi watched the reunion and squeezed her now empty hands together. It had felt nice to hold him, even for a minute.

Once their reunion was complete, the woman and her son walked towards Andi. "Thank you," she said. "He just ran ahead on the path and the next thing I knew..."

"It was no problem," Andi said. "I'm glad I was here when he needed me."

"At least this one isn't walking yet," the woman said.

Andi felt her chest tighten with the familiar pain as she looked at the baby. She knew it was socially acceptable to ask how old the baby was, or even what her name was. Instead, Andi managed a smile and said, "You're very lucky."

"I'm Sarah." The woman extended her hand.

"Andi." She took the woman's hand but couldn't tear her gaze away from the sleeping infant. She must have been about six months old. She would know if she asked. But she couldn't. She didn't want to know. Not really.

"Sarah? Noah?"

Both women turned towards the voice as a man came running down the path towards them.

"Dad!"

Noah tore away from his mom and ran full force to his dad, who swept him up in a big hug.

"I'm glad I could help," Andi said again, and excused herself from the happy scene.

"It was nice to meet you," Sarah called after her and smiled one more time before turning and joining in a family hug.

Andi walked as fast as she could, leaving their voices far behind her. Paige would have been a few months older than that baby. They would have been celebrating her first Christmas as a family.

She couldn't stop the thoughts from forming. But as soon as they did, she wished them away. The fact was, she would never know what Paige would have looked like if she'd lived, and there would never be a happy family scene for them. She was alone, and the sooner she accepted it, the easier it would be. She sniffed hard and wiped her gloved hand across her face.

I refuse to think about it this week, she thought to herself, as if willing her brain to cooperate with her heart would make a difference this time.

HE SHOULD HAVE WAITED for her, Colin thought for the hundredth time. Or at least left a note. He'd struggled with the proper way to handle leaving the villa earlier. He hadn't wanted to disturb her while she was in her room. He'd been more than pleasantly surprised that she'd agreed to stay, but he didn't want to make it weird for her.

After Andi had disappeared to her room, Colin, feeling

awkward and unsure of what to do next, decided to go over to the main building to explore a bit. He'd only been gone an hour when he went back to see if she'd like to have dinner with him. But finding her gone, he went back to the Lodge, hoping to find her. It was probably a bit on the desperate side, and completely out of character for him to chase after a woman, but there was something about her.

Trying not to look like he was waiting for someone, Colin chose a large wingback chair close to the fire that had a perfect view of the main doors. He flicked through a magazine, but didn't bother glancing at it. The Lodge was busy with people coming and going in different directions, no doubt to one of the many events or activities offered. Colin had picked up a schedule and chatted with Carmen earlier, who, as it turned out, was also the social director. Rose had been right; from a quick look at everything they had planned for the week, Castle Mountain Lodge was the perfect place to enjoy Christmas. There was everything from gingerbread house building to sleigh rides. Colin looked closely at the itinerary for that one. He could imagine that snuggling up to Andi, under a warm blanket, while riding through the pines, would be the perfect way to spend an evening.

He sighed, tossed the magazine aside and stood. He had to stop thinking of her that way. But the truth was, ever since seeing her in the lobby, he couldn't stop thinking of her like that. Wrong or not. Stretching his arms over his head, he turned and looked out the window. Before he could berate himself yet again for his poor decision to leave Andi alone, he caught a glimpse through the window of a woman who looked a lot like her. She was bundled up against the weather, but he knew. It was her.

Colin moved across the main room quickly and reached the side door at the exact moment Andi opened it. A blast of winter air preceded her.

"Andi," he said. "I was wondering where you went."

Did he really just say that? Colin inwardly cringed at his eagerness.

"Oh, hi." She looked up at him. Her face was flushed from the cold, crystals of ice formed on her eyelashes, and the very tip of her nose was red. He surprised himself by wanting to bend and kiss it, to feel the coolness on his lips.

But something was wrong. She looked distracted or upset. He couldn't tell which. Female emotions had never been his strong suit. "Are you okay?" By instinct, he took her arm and led her towards a group of chairs. She went willingly, but shook her head in protest.

"No," she said. "I mean, yes. I'm fine. Nothing happened. I went for a walk to get some fresh air, and I probably just stayed outside a little too long." She pulled the knit cap off her head and fluffed out her hair. "It's beautiful out there," she said and when she looked up again, any trace of sadness there might have been was gone.

"I don't know about beautiful," he said. "But definitely cold. Can I buy you a hot drink to warm up?"

She smiled and unzipped her thick coat. "I think I'd like that, thank you."

Together they walked down the long, open hallway that led away from the main room. There was a variety of gift shops lining one side of the corridor. Each shop held the usual t-shirts and coffee mugs emblazoned with pictures of the Canadian Rockies or wild animals. Things Colin used to find cheesy and tacky, but after being gone for so long, he could appreciate why visitors wanted to take a bit of Canada home with them.

They walked until they reached a small cafe-type of restaurant. "I know there are a few more choices in the village, but this looks nice," Colin said.

"I don't want to go outside again, if it's all the same to you."

"Here it is, then." Colin led them into the dim room and to a table near the fireplace.

After the waitress took their orders—a hot chocolate with Baileys for her, a beer for him—they settled into their chairs and looked at each other.

"Why does this feel like a first date?" Andi asked after a moment. She laughed, but Colin couldn't help wishing it was a first date. Or any date at all.

"You think so?"

"Well," she said with a smile. "I guess we've moved past the whole first date stage. Since we're staying together and all."

She tried to look confident, but Colin noticed her look away and she wouldn't meet his gaze. Could she be nervous about their arrangement? Or their shared history?

Lord knows he was, but only because of the intense attraction he had for her from the moment he met her. He wanted to ask her about Blaine—there was a lot of history between them—and he didn't know if it was a good idea to get involved with one of Blaine's exes.

Instead of asking what he really wanted to, he said, "Since we kind of skipped the first date, we should probably ask each other those awkward first date type questions. Don't you think?"

She looked up at him and Colin was rewarded with another smile. She relaxed into her chair and said, "Why not? Let me start."

"Absolutely, ladies first."

"I think the obvious question is, why are you here by yourself?"

So, she wasn't going to pull any punches, Colin thought.

"I mean, it's Christmas," Andi continued. "Why would you come to the mountains alone? Don't you have family?"

"Don't you?"

She sat back in her chair and crossed her arms. The smile

faded. "It's your turn," she said. "Besides, we already talked about my family."

"Okay," he said. "I came to Castle Mountain because I was told it the best place around to experience everything the holidays has to offer. I wanted it all. The whole Christmas experience."

"You haven't had it?"

"Not since I was a kid," Colin said truthfully. "I've missed it."

"Well, I think the whole holiday thing is for kids anyway," Andi said, her voice laced with bitterness. "I didn't realize there would be so many families up here. Shouldn't they all be at home wrapping gifts and decorating trees and all that?"

Before Colin could ask her what she had against Christmas, or families for that matter, the waitress arrived with their drinks. She placed a large mug of hot chocolate topped with a mountain of whipped cream and a cherry in front of Andi and a bottle of beer in front of him. When she left, the tension in the air had dissipated a little.

"You know I'm going to ask why you're here," he said.

"I told you earlier, my party planning company was offered a promo invitation. We've been wanting to check out the Lodge for a while. It's a great spot for weddings and large company functions and—"

"You thought Christmas would be the best time to conduct your research?"

"I did." She pulled her mug toward her and plucked the cherry from the top of her drink.

"You didn't want to spend it with your family? Those step-brothers you mentioned earlier?" Or Blaine, he'd wanted to add.

She sucked the cherry into her mouth, licking it clean while she considered the question. Colin had to look away.

"More like they didn't want to spend it with me," she said. Her voice was so soft and vulnerable, Colin looked back. The air of confidence she'd worn earlier was gone, but she didn't look sad either. "Eva, my business partner, didn't need me at work, so here I am."

Her quiet acceptance of her situation drew him, but he knew there was more to it. Colin couldn't remember the last time he'd met a woman as interesting as Andi. She was a mystery, one that he was looking forward to unraveling. He watched her for a minute while she sipped at her drink. When she looked up again, there was a thin line of whipped cream over her mouth.

"Well, Andi. So far, I know that you don't think much of Christmas," he said and leaned forward in his chair. "I also know that I plan to change that, because now that you've run into me, you're no longer going to be alone for the holidays." He reached out with his finger and with a gentle touch, wiped the cream off her lip.

It was a bold move, something he wouldn't normally do. But he also wasn't normally faced with such an unusual circumstance. Instinct told him bold was necessary; the intensity and heat behind Andi's gaze told him he was right.

*T*he morning dawned bright and clear. Andi stretched in her bed, rolled over and looked out the large picture window. The view was magnificent. The snow from the night before blanketed the trees, sparkling like gemstones in the morning sun.

Andi could have just lay there wrapped in her down comforter all morning, and was contemplating how to get a cup of coffee without actually moving, when there was a knock at the door.

"Good morning." Colin's voice came from the other side. "Are you awake?"

"I am. You can come in."

The door opened a crack. "I don't want to bug you."

"You kind of already did," Andi said with a smile. She hauled herself up to a sitting position and let her blankets fall. A moment too late, she realized she was wearing her faded Bugs Bunny t-shirt, her sleepwear of choice since Blaine left.

Colin moved slowly, like he was unsure if he should even be in her bedroom. His sandy hair was still damp, and he smelled fresh, yet musky in that way men did when they had just stepped out of the shower. He held a mug of coffee in his hand.

"I wasn't sure how you took it, so I guessed," he said before handing it to her.

Andi wrapped her hands around the mug and inhaled the rich aroma deeply. "Am I still dreaming?"

"Why do you say that?"

"I think you read my mind." She took a tentative sip. "Sugar," she said. "No cream." She looked at Colin, who was grinning like he'd just won the lottery.

"Like I said, I guessed. Did I get it right?"

Andi took another sip and said, "Close. I like it a little sweeter. But really close, thank you."

What were the odds he knew how she liked her coffee? Andi didn't think Blaine had known how she took it, and they'd shared more than one cup together in the past.

Banishing thoughts of her ex, she said to Colin, "I was just laying here thinking how much I'd love a coffee while I enjoyed the view and then you showed up. Are you a mind reader?"

Colin laughed and gestured to the corner of the bed. "May I?" he asked.

When she nodded, he sat down opposite from where she lay. It was a king-sized bed, and he was quite far away, but his proximity sent shivers through her body.

"This is weird, isn't it?" Colin said.

"Being here in this villa with my ex's friend? Or the fact that you're sitting on my bed while I'm wearing the lamest pajamas ever?"

"Both, I guess." He laughed. "And I like your pajamas, but I must admit, I'm a closet Bugs Bunny fan."

Andi smiled. "It's not weird. At least not anymore," she said and meant it.

Of course, she did still think the circumstances of their

accommodations were less than normal. And the fact that she was going to spend the holiday season with a guy she just met was also not typical. And she was going to stay. She'd decided last night that even if the roads were cleared, she'd stay. There was nothing waiting for her at home and after talking over drinks and dinner well into the wee hours the night before, she felt okay with it all. Better than okay. She liked the idea. And she liked Colin. He was genuinely funny and kind. He made her laugh over stories of his childhood growing up in Sparwood, a small town in the mountains, and told her all about how he'd spent the last few years working and traveling in the Caribbean, installing alarm systems for his own company, which explained his amazing tan in the middle of winter. It also explained how he could afford an entire villa to himself. The one subject they'd both avoided was Blaine. And that was okay with her.

"Well, I'm glad," he said, bringing her back to their conversation. "Because I have plans for today. That is, assuming you don't have anything else to do."

"Turns out my calendar is totally open."

"Good," Colin said. "Because I've been thinking about what you said last night. About not liking Christmas."

The smile faded from her face.

"It's not that I don't like Christmas," she said warily.

"You said it was for kids. But over the next few days, I plan to show you that Christmas can be just as much fun, if not more so, for adults too."

"I don't know."

"You said yourself you had nothing to do today," Colin said with a grin. "So get ready. We need to leave in an hour."

Before she could think of a valid argument, her cell phone rang. Taking the opportunity she grabbed it off the nightstand and glanced at the caller ID. "It's my mom," she said to Colin. "I should take it."

"I'll wait outside," he said and stood up. "Remember, one hour."

"Don't count on it," she said, but he was already gone.

Andi sighed and clicked on her phone.

"Hi, Mom."

"Andi." Her mother's voice came on the line. The connection crackled and there was an echo. She must have found a pay phone somewhere. "Merry Christmas, sweetie."

"Thanks. Where are you?"

"We're in the cutest little town on the coast of Costa Rica. Just here for the day, though. The ship sails at five."

"It sounds lovely," Andi said. "And hot."

"I just wanted to see how you're holding up today. It's Blaine's party tonight, isn't it?"

Leave it to her mom to remember the details. Of course last year, she'd attended the party as well. After all, they'd all been practically family.

"I guess it is today," Andi said. She'd managed to put it out of her head.

"It'll be okay, sweetie. I promise. At least you'll be with your father and his new family for Christmas." Andi couldn't bring herself to tell her mother the truth. There was no point in having her worry about her during the holidays. "Make sure you give those adorable boys a hug for me. Whatever I have to say about their dad, they are sweet kids."

"Yes they are," Andi agreed.

For the next few minutes, she half listened while her mom described the villages they'd visited and the snorkeling trip Val had talked her into. Andi looked around her room, at the snowy scenery outside and her thoughts drifted to Colin.

What was the harm? she thought. Why not spend the day with him? It's not like she had anything else to do. Besides, it would beat sitting in her room with the overwhelming sensation of loneliness pressing down on her.

"Mom," Andi interrupted her mother's description of the beach. "I'm sorry but I have to run."

"No trouble, sweetie. You have a merry Christmas and I'll give you a call as soon as we get home."

"Thanks, Mom. I love you and hugs to Val, too."

As soon as she hung up, Andi got up and stood, facing her large, empty bed. There really was nothing left to lose.

## 6

*W*alking down the path, Andi tried to figure out where Colin was taking her. If she was being honest with herself, she did enjoy the mystery, even if it was centered around Christmas.

"I hope I'm dressed okay," she said. Not knowing what he had planned for her, Andi had dressed simply in jeans and a long-sleeved shirt, and grabbed a thick wool sweater to layer with. Her hair was tucked under a cap and she wore matching gloves.

He glanced in her direction as they walked and his eyes traveled over her. "You look fantastic," he said.

She smiled at the compliment. "But, am I dressed appropriately for what we're doing?" She tried again to get him to tell her.

"Nice try," he said. "I told you, you're just going to have to wait and see."

She sighed, trying to pretend that not knowing bothered her, but secretly she liked it. Andi couldn't remember a man ever taking charge and planning a whole day for her. She might even have thought it romantic in another situation.

"I missed the snow," Colin said, changing the subject. "It's funny, snow isn't something you think you're going to miss, but I did. It's beautiful."

"It is," she said. She looked at him out of the corner of her eye. "But I bet being surrounded by sand and sun was a pretty good consolation prize."

"It was at first." He kicked at a snowdrift as they walked.

"How long were you there?"

"Five years," he said. "Everywhere from the British Virgin Islands to St. Lucia. I got around."

"And no girlfriend in any of those places?"

"Nope," he said. "None. I told you, relationships aren't my thing." He kept his voice casual, but she noticed the frown.

"How come I don't believe you?"

He stopped then and looked at her. "You really want to know?" She instinctively pulled back at the shift of tone in his voice. His warm smile had vanished.

She swallowed hard and answered, "Yes. I do."

For a moment, she didn't think he would tell her and then he said, "I was engaged to be married once. I loved her. That was, until she got pregnant with some other guy's child."

She reached for him but he pulled back. "That's an awful story."

"Well, like I said before, relationships are more trouble than they're worth."

"Tell me about it," she muttered.

"Are you going to tell me about Blaine?"

She wasn't surprised that he'd finally asked. If anything, she was impressed that it took him so long to ask her. "There's nothing to tell," she said. "It didn't work out. End of story."

"That's it?" Colin looked at her, his eyes searching for something.

"That's it," she said.

His gaze grew more intense. It held her and for a moment, Andi forgot they were supposed to be on their way to a fun day of distraction.

Breaking away from his stare, she did her best to keep her voice light, and she asked, "Now, don't you have something you're supposed to show me?"

Playing along, Colin didn't miss a beat. "Oh, I can think of a few things I'd like to—"

Andi cut him off by giving him a playful shove.

She must have pushed him harder than she thought, because Colin stumbled off the path, put his foot down deep in the drift and tripped up to his knees in snow.

He looked up at her, his face a mask of seriousness.

"Oh, I'm sorry," she said quickly and reached to give him a hand. "I didn't mean to—"

He took hold of her hand and yanked her off the path and into the snow with him.

"Oops," he said with a laugh. "I didn't mean to do that."

Andi landed on her stomach and just barely missed having a face full of snow. She could hear Colin laughing behind her, so once she got over the shock of being flung into the cold, she quickly pulled her hands toward her, scooping up as much snow as possible in the process. Before he had a chance to react, she rolled to her back and flung the snow up into his face.

His laughter stopped. She watched from her position while he wiped his face. "So," he said slowly. "That's the way you want to play."

Like a little boy, his face split into a grin and Andi knew if she didn't move quickly, there would be trouble. She pushed herself to her feet as best she could in the deep snow and started running and stumbling through the trees. "Give me a head start," she called behind her.

"You think so?" Colin laughed, and the deep sound filled the forest around her, making her laugh too.

The snow was deep, past her knees, which made running difficult. Her heart raced from the excitement of the chase. She was just about to turn and check on Colin's proximity when a solid thud hit her from behind.

Andi closed her eyes and braced herself for the impact to follow. But instead of shoving her face first into the snow, Colin's arms wrapped around her waist, cradling her. Together they fell to the ground, lying side by side.

"Got you," he said.

She opened her eyes to find his face only inches away from hers. "Yes, you did."

"No fair," she said when she had some control. "Your legs are way longer than mine."

"That's not my fault," he said. "It was a valiant attempt at escape, though."

His breath smelled like cinnamon and coffee. Andi's stomach flipped when he moved closer to her in the snow and put his hand on her hip. Even through the layers of wool, his touch burned her, lighting something inside.

"Colin," she started to say, "I—"

"You're going to be soaked soon," he said abruptly. In the next instant, his hand was gone and he was jumping up, pulling her out of the snow. "I'm sorry," he said. "I should have thought about it. Are you cold?"

Andi busied herself with brushing snow from her body because it was easier than looking him in the eye. Had he been about to kiss her?

"I'm fine," she said. "Honestly." Andi looked up. "Besides," she said. "Next time, you're going down."

He laughed and took Andi's hand, leading her out of the

snowdrift and back to the path. "We'll see. But for now, let's get started on the festive fun."

For a while, they walked without speaking. It was a comfortable silence and he held on to her hand. Andi tried not to think about the almost kiss that wasn't. The last thing she needed in her life was a man, especially this one. Eva would tell her she was being crazy, and she absolutely needed a man, at least for a night or two. But Eva was like that. Andi wasn't. Her relationships were long-term. Before Blaine, there had only been one other serious boyfriend and a series of dates that didn't lead anywhere. She liked commitment, and she wasn't ready for that. Besides, Colin had made it quite clear that he had no room for relationships either.

Saving her from her thoughts, Colin broke the silence. "Remember that I told you I was going to do my best to change your mind about Christmas?"

Andi nodded and gave him a sidelong glance. "Yes, but be warned. I'm not going to be an easy convert."

"I like a challenge." He ran a hand through his hair but his eyes never left hers. They blazed with intensity and a challenge of their own, and Andi had to look away.

"So are you going to tell me where we're going, or what?"

"I don't have to," he said. "We're here." Distracted by her thoughts, Andi hadn't noticed that they'd made their way out of the woods into the main courtyard of the Lodge. In the middle of the clearing was a large frozen pond where ice skaters swirled and glided around the surface. Benches were placed at one end of the ice and there was a hut set up where staff members were handing out skates to guests. Christmas songs, piped from hidden speakers, filled the air.

To Andi's horror, Colin took her hand and led her in the direction of the hut. "First on the celebrate Christmas plan is ice skating," he announced.

Andi came to an abrupt halt, her boots jamming into the snow. Colin, still with a grip on her hand, continued to walk forward, jarring her.

"Andi, what's wrong?"

"I don't skate," Andi said.

He started to tease her, and was going to tell her she was being ridiculous, but then he saw the look in her eyes. She was scared. It didn't take a genius to see the way she watched the ice as if it were about to crack open and swallow her. He never considered that she might not know how to skate.

"It's okay," Colin said, keeping his voice gentle. "I promise nothing bad will happen."

"The last time I put on skates I was six years old and these older kids convinced me to play this stupid game."

"Let me guess," Colin said, trying not to smile. "Crack the whip?"

"That's it," Andi said. She started waving her arms in the air. "I went flying across the ice and flew right off the edge."

He couldn't help it; he couldn't stifle his laugh any longer. Andi glared at him, but he caught her smile when she turned away.

"Fine," she said after a moment. "Let's do it."

Colin swallowed his laughter. "Really?"

"Of course," she said, and headed towards the ice. "I might not like it, but I'm not afraid to try something new."

I certainly hope not, Colin thought. He followed after her, staying just a few steps behind so he could enjoy the view.

Lying in the bed the night before, he'd come up with the idea of converting Andi into a Christmas lover. It served two purposes for him. One, he'd have company for his much anticipated Christmas back in Canada, and two, he'd be able to spend more time with a gorgeous woman. He hated to admit it, even to himself, but having an excuse to be with Andi was the most important reason. Every moment with her was comfortable and more enjoyable than the last. And hearing that things were totally over between her and Blaine—well, that was just a bonus. It was turning out to be a much better holiday than he could have imagined.

They retrieved some skates from the hut and found an empty bench to get ready.

"What?" she said, catching him staring at her. "Don't make fun of me because I don't know how to tie these up." She held up a skate and looked at it hopelessly.

Colin slid off the bench and knelt in the snow in front of her. "You've really never skated except for that one time?" He took the skate out of her hand. "Didn't you say you were Canadian?"

He took her boot off and held her foot lightly in one hand, while he tucked it under the bench.

"That's stereotypical," she said. "Just because I'm Canadian, I'm expected to know how to skate?"

"Of course," Colin said, while he gently pushed the skate onto her foot. "We're also supposed to know all the hockey teams, eat poutine, and be able to build an igloo." He was rewarded with her warm laughter. She hadn't said anything, but Colin had the impression that she didn't laugh enough. She was funny and warm, but there was something sad inside as well. He was enjoying bringing the happiness out in her.

"Just to warn you," she said. "I'm horribly unbalanced. I'll probably fall a thousand times and I may need to lean on you."

Colin pulled the laces of her skate tight and looked up at her. His voice was serious when he said, "You can lean on me all you like."

He, in fact, was hoping she would lean on him, and let him

wrap his arms around her and maybe even get that kiss he should have gone for when they were lying in the snow. And then, maybe, well, who knew where a kiss could lead? After seeing her wearing nothing but a thin t-shirt earlier, he couldn't get the image of her in bed out of his head. He was only human after all, and he'd definitely like to see that again, only next time without the t-shirt.

Before he could let his thoughts get carried away, Colin grabbed the other skate and put it on for her, tying it with expert hands. "Just give me a second while I get mine on," he said when he was done.

As quickly as he could, he moved to where he'd left his skates and started tugging them on. Out of the corner of his eye, he saw Andi push up from the bench and wobble on the blades.

"Just wait, Andi," he said. "I'll be right there. You don't want to fall if you're not comfortable."

"No," she said. "I got this. I'm sure it can't be—"

He watched in horror as both Andi's feet flew out from under her. Arms waving wildly, she tried desperately to right herself. With a small shriek, she landed hard, flat on her back.

Colin jumped up and skated over the ice to where Andi sat. She was staring straight ahead, but wasn't crying. That was a good sign.

"Andi," he said, dropping down next to her. "Are you okay? Can you wiggle your legs?"

She turned slowly and looked at him as if he'd lost his mind.

"Where does it hurt?"

Andi tipped her head, blinked once and a cross between a laugh and a snort burst from her throat.

It took Colin a second to realize she was laughing not crying, but when he did, he shook his head. "Come on," he said and reached out. "Get up."

She grabbed his hand and he hoisted her to her feet. Afraid

she would fall again, he held her around the waist. "Are you okay?"

She wiped at her face where tears had started to leak out her eyes. "I'll be fine," she said as her laughter died down. "There's going to be a bruise, and of course I feel like an idiot. But hey, if you can't laugh about it..."

"It did look pretty funny," Colin said. "Something out of a cartoon. But you're lucky you didn't break your tailbone."

"Nope, not broken." She rubbed her bottom and then looked up at him with a smile. "So, are you going to teach me how to do this right?"

"I promise," he said and took her hands. "You'll be skating like a pro in no time." Colin spun her slowly in a circle with him. "Or at least you won't fall down, anyway."

As soon as he was ready, Colin led her back to the pond. She was nervous at first, understandably so after her crash, but Colin took her slowly along the ice. He dodged all the children who were flying across the surface as if they'd been born on skates. Occasionally, one would fall, and Colin had to do a quick duck around them, leading Andi safely away.

After a few laps around the pond, Andi said, "Okay, I think I can do it on my own."

"Are you sure?" Colin didn't think she would fall again, but he didn't want to let go of her hand. He liked the way it felt in his. It fit.

She nodded, her mouth fixed in a determined line. He was learning quickly that she was pretty stubborn. If she wanted to skate, she would.

"Okay," he said and released her hand. "I'll stay close. Just in case."

Her face still fixed in concentration, Andi pushed ahead with her right foot. Then, she slowly slid her left foot up. She did it a few more times. Shuffling awkwardly across the ice, Andi managed to move a few feet. "I'm doing it," she cried and spun herself around so quickly, she would have lost her balance if Colin hadn't reached out and grabbed her around the waist again.

"Got you."

"Yes you do," she whispered. Her voice was husky and incredibly sexy.

He should have kissed her then. Her lips were only inches from him. He only had to bend down and they would meet. The flush on her cheeks—was it from desire or the exertion of skating? Would she respond? Or would he ruin their holiday together?

"You should try again," he said and pulled away from her, releasing her waist.

He heard her sigh, or at least he thought he did, and she turned away from him, putting her arms out to her sides. Andi resumed her skate-shuffle and after a few steps, she started lengthening her stride and even gliding a little.

"You're doing great," Colin said. He skated beside her. Close enough to help, but not too close. The urge to grab her, kiss her deep and put a real flush in her face was strong. But as much as he wanted to, he couldn't risk making their arrangement awkward. He was finally having a traditional Christmas, and enjoying it. That would disappear, and so would she, if Andi didn't reciprocate his feelings. Besides, the last thing he needed was a relationship, and Andi was definitely not a one-night stand type of girl.

Together they skated around the pond and after a few more laps, Colin said, "How about a break?"

"No way," Andi said and quickened her pace. She had improved at a remarkable rate. "I'm doing awesome. This is so fun." She smiled and turned to look at him but in the process lost her balance and wobbled on her blades. Her face returned to a mask of concentration and within seconds she'd regained her composure. "Don't tell me you're getting tired?" She didn't turn to look at him, focusing instead on what she was doing.

"Not tired," he said. "But thirsty. Besides, we have more planned for today."

"We do?" she said.

"Of course. You didn't really think this was it, did you?"

She smiled, but didn't take her gaze off the ice.

"I'll tell you what—I'll go find us some water. You make a couple more laps."

"Thanks, Colin. I'll be fine. Honestly."

He laughed and watched her go ahead. He almost followed her again; the draw towards Andi was undeniably strong. But he didn't want to appear too eager, so after a few moments, he turned and skated towards the bench where he'd left his shoes.

Colin sat down on the bench next to another man taking his skates off.

"Your wife's first time on skates?" the man asked.

Colin looked over at him while he undid the laces. "Yeah," he said, not bothering to correct him. "Can you believe she hasn't skated since she was a kid?"

"Well she seems to be doing pretty good now," the man said. "I'm Kirk by the way." He extended his hand which Colin took. "I'm up here with my family. We just taught my son to skate, too."

Colin looked to where he pointed; a woman was loading a baby into a sleigh wagon while a little boy made snow angels. "Did he like it?" he asked.

Kirk laughed. "He did, but I think he liked the promise of hot chocolate after even more."

Colin tugged his first skate off. "I'd have to agree with him. Hot chocolate sounds good."

"Hey, why don't you two join us?"

Colin looked over to Andi, who was still doggedly skating around the pond. He smiled at her dedication. For a woman who hadn't wanted to try it, she really seemed to like it.

"The Lodge was going to set up a big bonfire down by the toboggan hill later," Kirk said. "According to my wife, there'll be hot chocolate, apple cider, and snacks. Should be nice."

Colin took another glance at Andi before looking back at Kirk. "It does sound nice. I don't remember seeing that on the schedule they gave me at the front desk yesterday."

"Apparently, that schedule of events is out the window."

"What do you mean? I thought this place had the best Christmas activities around. Better than the North Pole, even."

Kirk pulled his boot on and grabbed his skates. "They do. We come here every year for the holidays. But from what I understand, the event coordinator up and quit yesterday. So, they're winging it. So far so good, though."

"Sounds like it," Colin said and turned his attention to his other skate. "That's really too bad, though. I had a whole thing planned for us for the next few days."

"Well, like I said, they're still going to have stuff going on. But Carmen at the desk was pretty frazzled when I saw her earlier." Kirk stood. "Anyway, I should get going. But maybe we'll see you guys later? The kids are great, but some adult company would be good, too. I'm sure our wives would get along."

Colin was about to tell him that Andi wasn't his wife, but something stopped him. "Yeah," he said. "We'll see you later. Hot chocolate sounds perfect. Besides, I have to rethink my itinerary as it turns out."

Kirk laughed and returned to his family. Colin watched him kiss his wife on the cheek and ruffle the boy's hair. Something in his chest tweaked. It couldn't be envy. There was no way he wanted the happy family lifestyle. Colin hadn't given relationships much thought since the mess with his ex. Over the years, he'd learned it was so much easier not to get too deeply involved with women. Anything longer than a week was reason for trouble.

Besides, whenever he thought of what a healthy, loving relationship should be like, he thought of his parents. Since they were teenagers, they'd been deeply in love, and every day of their life together, they didn't hesitate to show it. But when his mom died unexpectedly in a car accident, sixteen-year-old Colin watched while his father deteriorated and threw himself into work until he was a different person altogether. He might as well have been an orphan. It wasn't until two years later, when Colin moved out, that he lost his father officially. His dad had never been able to heal after losing the love of his life and finally he just gave up. How could someone love another person so much that they simply chose not to live without them? Colin couldn't understand it. Nor did he ever want to experience it.

But he couldn't deny that seeing Kirk and his family together sparked something in him. Maybe at thirty-five, things were finally changing?

"Hey," Andi said as she skated towards him. Colin looked up just in time to catch her as she crashed into him, toppling Colin and the bench. Andi landed on top of him, knocking the air out of him. He expected her to be apologetic and tripping over herself with embarrassment. Instead she broke into laughter.

"Good catch," she managed to get out. "I have a little problem with stopping."

It took Colin a moment to get his breath back with her weight on top of him. When he was able to, he said, "Having fun?" He grabbed her around the waist and hoisted her to the side and off him.

"I am. This is great. We'll have to do this again."

Colin stood and pulled Andi to her unsteady feet. "Absolutely. We can come back and skate again." As soon as the words left his mouth, he swallowed hard. He shouldn't have assumed she'd want to spend more time with him. After all, she was here on her own holiday too. "If you want to, that is," he added quickly.

"Are you kidding? Of course I want to." She sat down on the bench that Colin had righted, and started unlacing her skates. "I'll kick your butt next time." She laughed.

"You have an amazing laugh," he said, and before she could respond, he added, "Here, let me help you." Colin dropped to his knees and expertly unlaced Andi's skates.

"So, what's next?" Andi said.

"Oh, so now you're into this mission I have to make you enjoy Christmas?"

She shook her head. "I wouldn't say that," she said. "In fact, I still don't think that ice skating qualifies as a festive activity. But it was fun. So if you have anything else equally fun planned, then I'm game."

## 7

*A*ndi looked up at Colin as they walked into the clearing. "Okay, this is over the top Christmasy."

The fire was roaring and situated among the pine trees. Picnic tables had been cleared of snow and were clustered at one end of the fire. They held thermos of hot chocolate, apple cider, and an array of snacks and toppings for the drinks. Log benches encircled the fire, occupied by adults and children alike. A man playing the guitar sat on a log, strumming carols that the group was singing along to as they sipped their drinks.

"You'll enjoy it, I promise," Colin said and squeezed her hand again.

Every time he did that, it sent a thrill through her. She loved the feel of his hand in hers. It felt like it belonged there. She would happily hold his hand all day. And if that meant going along with his crazy plan to convert her into a fan of the holidays, she'd go with it. The time she'd spent with Colin had been the most enjoyable she'd had in a while and she wasn't in a hurry to stop it.

"We'll see," she said.

"Hey, Colin," a man said, noticing them as they made their way to the tables.

"Kirk." Colin let go of her hand and reached out to shake the man's hand. He was wearing a baby strapped to his chest in a Snuggly. A baby in a pink snowsuit. Andi's stomach flipped.

"You two know each other?" she asked.

"Well, not really," Colin said. "We met back at the pond." He turned to Kirk again and said, "Kirk, this is Andi."

"It's nice to meet you. Come meet my wife," Kirk said, as he shook her hand. "There's tons of room at the fire."

Andi glanced over at Colin, who shrugged. She didn't want to spend time with strangers, especially if they included a baby, but she didn't want to be rude either, so she followed Colin's lead and went with him to the fire.

"Sarah, this is Colin and his wife, Andi."

Wife? Andi looked up at Colin, who had the decency to blush and offer a sheepish smile. When he didn't correct the man, Andi turned to the woman who'd just stood from the bench.

"Hi," she said.

"It's you," Sarah said. "What a nice surprise. Kirk told me about meeting your husband, but I had no idea it was you."

Again, Andi shot Colin a look before turning and smiling warmly at Sarah.

"You've met?" Kirk asked.

"We met last night," Andi said.

"She was the woman who helped Noah when he got lost."

"I thought you looked familiar," Kirk said. "Sorry I didn't recognize you. It was pretty dark. Thank you for helping our son."

Andi nodded. She remembered the happy family scene vividly. Sarah seemed like a nice woman, but the proximity of the baby was unsettling and she kept her body turned slightly away.

"Where is Noah?" Colin asked. "I'd like to congratulate him on his first time skating."

He liked kids? Andi felt something inside her stir. She couldn't remember Blaine ever asking about a child before. Sure, he'd been excited about their pregnancy, but he'd never gone out of his way to befriend anyone else's child. Not that it mattered, she told herself. She wasn't in a relationship with Colin. And she didn't have children. It didn't matter.

"That's so sweet," Sarah said. "He's playing reindeer games in the field with some of the other kids."

"Reindeer games?" Andi asked. Things were looking more Christmasy by the second.

Sarah nodded. "Isn't it great? They've thought of everything up here. It's the perfect place for families."

Andi tried to smile. She hadn't considered that fact when she'd fled to the mountains.

"Why don't you two sit?" Kirk said. "Colin and I can grab some drinks."

"Hot chocolate okay?" Colin asked.

Andi nodded numbly and squeezed onto the bench where Sarah pointed.

The fire was hot even from her position a few feet away and it only took a few seconds before she was warmed through and had to take her gloves and hat off.

"Isn't it funny that our husbands found each other?" Sarah asked. She was excited, and from only the few minutes Andi had chatted with her, she could tell that Sarah was one of those people who was genuinely happy and sweet. Andi wouldn't be responsible for ruining her mood.

"I think it's great," Andi said, with as much sincerity as she could muster.

"Almost like we were meant to be friends," Sarah said. "You know, I just love coming up here for the holidays, but it's always nice to meet new people."

Andi stared into the flames. "How long have you been here?"

"Oh, only a few days. We're leaving on Boxing Day to spend some time with Kirk's family. All of mine are out East. We could fly out to see them, but it's become a bit of a tradition for us to come here. And I think traditions are so important for young families, don't you?"

"We don't have children." Andi swallowed hard.

"Well, there's plenty of time for that yet," Sarah said. "The two of you look so in love and cute together. I understand wanting to wait. You can never get those years back. Not that I'd trade it now, of course."

"Of course," Andi agreed. Sarah continued to talk about her kids and how wonderful they were, but Andi only half listened. Her mind was still on the comment Sarah had made about how she and Colin looked to be so in love. What would she think if she knew that they barely knew each other?

Before Andi could dwell on it any further, the guys returned with mugs of hot chocolate. "I was just telling Andi how you two have plenty of time to think about having kids," Sarah said.

"Oh were you?" Colin said.

"Well, of course, I mentioned how wonderful they are and all that," Sarah said, looking to her husband.

"Of course," he agreed.

"But seeing another couple so in love and carefree like these two, well, I can't help but think of what it was like for us once," Sarah said.

Kirk leaned forward and kissed her on the lips. "We're still madly in love."

Colin slid onto the bench next to Andi and put his arm around her shoulders. Pulling her close, he said, "Well, I'm sure when the time is right, children will be a blessing to our love just like it has been for you two."

Andi would have shot him a glare if he'd been looking at her. Instead, she jabbed her elbow into his rib cage the best she could. In response, Colin pulled her closer into an embrace.

"But for now we're still having fun learning just as much as we can about each other," Colin said. "Isn't that right, darling?"

"Couldn't have said it better myself, pumpkin," she said.

"So, how long have you two been married?" Kirk asked. He unstrapped the baby, who had started to fuss, and handed her to Sarah.

"We're newlyweds."

"Two years."

They answered at the same time.

Kirk and Sarah exchanged confused glances, and Kirk asked, "You don't remember?"

Andi waited for Colin to explain. After all, it was his lie.

Saving him from answering, Carmen, from the front desk, spotted them from across the fire. She waved and started making her way through the crowd towards them. "Excuse us for a moment," he said. Colin took the hot chocolate from her hands, put it on the bench and pulled Andi to her feet.

Andi shrugged an apology and was still stifling her giggle as they walked towards Carmen.

"Mr. Hartford, Ms. Williams," Carmen said when they approached. "I just wanted to thank you again for being so understanding about the mix-up in the rooms."

"Oh, it's been fine," Andi said.

"More than fine," Colin added. "In fact, we've been enjoying a lot of the Lodge's activities together. I'm determined to show Ms. Williams how much fun Christmas can be."

Carmen smiled cautiously and glanced down at their clasped hands. "Well, it was most definitely a happy coincidence that the two of you had met before and I'm so glad it's all working out," she said. "I do wish we had more activities planned, but our event coordinator quit and left me in quite the situation."

"That's awful," Andi said. "But it looks like you're managing okay. This is a fabulous setup." She waved her arm to encompass the campfire.

"I've been fortunate with my staff," Carmen said. "They've really stepped up. But I'm just so upset that the Holly Berry Ball won't happen this year. It's just too much for me to take on, as well as running the desk, and it's such a shame because this year would have been our tenth anniversary."

"The Holly Berry Ball?" Andi asked.

"It's our annual Christmas Eve celebration. We've always prided ourselves on providing a family friendly dance to celebrate the holiday season. It's wonderful, but this year, I just don't think I can pull it off on my own. I know the children will be so disappointed."

For a moment, Andi was afraid the woman was going to cry. She was doing a good job keeping it together, but Andi couldn't help noticing the stray hairs escaping her barrettes, and the dark circles under her eyes. Isn't that what the holidays did to people? Turned them into big tightly wound balls of anxiety.

Her stomach turned, but Andi knew she didn't have a choice. Even though it was a holiday event, and the thought of organizing something as cutesy sounding as a Holly Berry Ball made her slightly queasy, she knew she wouldn't be able to live with herself if the event was canceled. Not when she knew she could help.

"Carmen," she said, before she stopped herself. "I think I can help."

"Really?" Carmen said. She looked like she might leap forward and kiss Andi.

"That's right," Colin added. "Andi runs a party planning business."

"And you really think you could help?" Carmen asked. "I mean, it's last minute and all. The ball is tomorrow."

Andi laughed and put her hand on the other woman's shoulder. "I'll tell you what," she said. "Let me see what you have so far and I'll make a few phone calls to my business partner. Last minute is her specialty. Don't worry, Carmen. I'll make it happen."

"Oh, Ms. Williams, thank you so much. You may have just saved my job."

"Please, just call me Andi."

"I'll have all the files sent to your villa right away," Carmen said and turned to leave, but turned around again and grabbed Andi's hand. "I'm so sorry," she said. "I didn't mean to dump this on you on your holiday. In fact, I was trying to find you both to tell you that because of our mix-up, we'd like to offer you a complimentary dinner tonight at Oliver's. It's our premier restaurant."

"Oh, that's very nice of you," Andi said. "But I may have too much work to do, and I don't want to assume that Colin will be free." She looked over at him.

"Nonsense," he said. "We'd love to take you up on your offer, Carmen. And I'll help Andi with anything she needs to get this ball organized. It'll be fun."

Andi smiled and looked at him. "You'll help?"

"Of course." Their eyes locked and something passed between them. Something that made Andi wish they were alone. She reached for his hand and squeezed it. An action that seemed so comfortable, and might even be normal in another circumstance. But normal or not, Andi liked the feel of her hand in his and the electricity that was passing between them.

"It's going to be great," Andi said. Her eyes didn't leave his and from somewhere in the distance, she thought she heard Carmen excuse herself, but still, she didn't look away. She dared him with her eyes to kiss her. He'd had his opportunity more than once today, but each time he pulled away. And despite all of her common sense telling her to look away, she couldn't. She hadn't used common sense since she'd arrived at the Lodge, and so far it was working out pretty good. But maybe she'd read the situation wrong. Maybe Colin wasn't interested in her that way at all.

There was only one way to find out, Andi thought. She might as well be the one to make the first move. She'd never been the wallflower type. And like Eva said, it could be good for her to have a fling. She raised herself to her toes and leaned in. "This is going to be a lot of work," she whispered, and inched closer. "Maybe a very late night."

"I like late nights," Colin said. His voice was husky, his breathing hard. Andi closed her eyes and bridged the last few inches between them, meeting his lips with her own.

The kiss was soft and tentative at first while they explored each other. When Colin wrapped his arm around her and pulled her even closer, any doubts she'd had were erased. She let herself sink into him. It had been so long since she'd been kissed and her body responded readily with a heat building in her core. Colin parted her lips gently with his tongue. He tasted sweet, like hot chocolate and peppermint.

It was over too soon, but she was well aware of their very public environment and if the kiss went on much longer, it might not be appropriate for all audiences. She pulled away and smiled when she saw the look in his eyes. There was no mistaking that he felt the same way.

"That was unexpected," Colin said.

She raised an eyebrow at him.

"Well," he amended. "Not entirely. I've been wanting to do

that almost from the moment I saw you."

She laughed. "So not unexpected at all, then."

He shook his head and Andi couldn't be sure, but it almost looked as if he blushed a little.

"Come on," she said. "If I'm going to get this ball organized, I better get started." Eva was going to kill her with the extra work the Holly Berry Ball would be, but it would be fun. And if Colin was helping, well, all of a sudden, the idea of planning a dreaded holiday party held a certain appeal.

COLIN LEFT Andi combing through the dozens of folders and files Carmen had sent to the villa and went to check out the shops that lined the courtyard and made up part of the Village. He hadn't packed anything beyond jeans, t-shirts, and sweaters, and from the look of the menu at Oliver's, going out for dinner was going to require a wardrobe modification.

There were a surprising number of stores to choose from, considering they were up in the mountains away from everything. But maybe that was the reason. A vacation destination with shopping built right in—a little something for everyone. The more time he spent at the Lodge, the more he enjoyed it. Or maybe it was just the company he'd enjoyed. Either way, it was turning out to be a great holiday.

It didn't take long for Colin to find a menswear store and he was soon outfitted with dress pants and a blue shirt the sales girl told him brought out the sparkle in his eyes. Of course, she'd been flirting with him and he surprised himself by not flirting back, like he normally would. Instead, he couldn't help but wonder what the sales girl would say if she knew it was Andi who'd put the sparkle in his eyes earlier. Or more specifically, the kiss they'd shared.

His cell phone rang as he headed outside, bags slung over his shoulder. He dug it out of his coat pocket and answered it without checking the ID. No doubt Andi wanted him to pick up something for the party, or needed him back at the villa. Maybe she just wanted him home. His heart raced at the thought.

"I'm on my way," he said into the phone.

"On your way where?" Rose's grandmotherly voice came through the line. "I thought you were holed up in the mountains, having a traditional holiday or some such thing. Why you couldn't get the same thing with my family is beyond me. There's nothing wrong with the way we do Christmas, ya know?"

Colin suppressed a laugh and rolled his eyes. Rose had worked overtime to get him to come to her house for the holidays. And as much as he wanted to experience everything the holidays had to offer, he couldn't imagine being surrounded by her fifteen grandchildren. Even for him, it would be a little too much.

"Merry Christmas, Rose," he said. "Shouldn't you be enjoying your family?"

"I'm doing just that," she said. "But I just had to call my favorite boss to see how he was doing. I worry about you in the mountains all by yourself."

"I'm not by myself." Colin knew Rose didn't approve of his playboy ways. She would love it if he would find a nice girl and settle down. He couldn't help wondering what she would think of Andi.

"Is that so?" He could almost see her wagging her finger at him. "Well, I guess there's nothing I can say to change your mind about turkey dinner then, is there?"

"Actually, Rose," he said. "It's not what you think." He wouldn't normally fill his assistant in on personal details, but Colin found himself telling her everything about Andi and the unlikely situation they were in. As he talked, he walked along the cobblestones, kicking at the snow that drifted across his path. The air was crisp, even with the sun high in the sky. It was the perfect weather for the end of December and he'd missed it. Too many years surrounded by the sandy beaches and blue ocean had made him long for the ice and snow. He didn't think it possible to miss the feeling of his toes going numb, or the ache in your back after shoveling the driveway, but he had.

When he had finished relaying the story, there was silence on the other end of the phone. "Rose? Are you still there?" The reception could be spotty in the mountains; maybe he'd lost the connection.

He heard a cough and then Rose's voice, much quieter than usual. "Colin, if I didn't know better, I'd say you were in love."

Colin tripped over his feet and dropped his bags in the snow. When he recovered, he said, "What are you talking about? Love? That's crazy."

"Is it?"

"Rose, you're being ridiculous. I just met this woman."

"Colin Hartford, I've been around the block a few times, and I know more about love than I'd care to admit," she said. "And I'll tell you what. You don't need weeks and months to fall in love; you just need the right two people and the perfect circumstance."

Colin brushed the snow off his bags, quickly checking to see if any had slipped inside. "Well, I don't know about that."

"Just keep an open heart," she said. "I have to run now. There are still more gifts to wrap before the madness starts."

"Have a happy holiday, Rose," Colin said with a smile. "I'll see you next week."

"Merry Christmas, Colin."

After he hung up, Colin couldn't focus his thoughts. In love? With Andi? He'd never heard anything so ridiculous. He didn't do relationships, let alone ones that involved actual love. And with Blaine's ex? There was no way. But if anyone could see it, it would be Rose.

She'd been a fabulous assistant to him and his father before him. She had known him since he was a child. He had to admit, she was probably the one person who knew him the best. After his father died and Colin decided to take over the alarm systems company, Rose had walked him through everything. She'd been indispensable. And so loyal. Even when his dad practically ran the business into the ground, she'd stayed with him, despite only barely making a wage herself. Colin had more than made up for that, though.

It wasn't until after he'd turned things around and built up the business again that Colin had the idea of expanding into the Caribbean. The decision to offer companies down south top-of-the line security had been a good one. Both Colin and Rose did well for themselves now. But he'd been gone a long time and it was no secret that Rose had wanted Colin to come home. But would he stay? Colin stopped walking, bent down and scooped up the snow in his bare hand. The icy coolness ran through his fingers as it melted. Yes, he was ready to take the snow over the sandy beaches.

A figure in a shop window caught his eye, distracting him from his thoughts. The store looked to be classier than the typical souvenir shop he'd seen earlier. There were ceramics, ornaments, and other beautiful handicrafts that even he could appreciate. But it was an item in the back of the window that'd made him stop.

Stuck on a shelf, towards the back of the display, was the perfect non-Christmasy Christmas gift for Andi. They hadn't said anything about exchanging presents. But it didn't seem right to have such a lovely tree in the villa with nothing under it. Besides, she wasn't a stranger anymore. She was Andi.

## 8

"*E*va, don't freak out." Andi tucked the phone under her chin and flipped through the file in front of her. "I may have a little project for us."

"Any conversation that starts like that is bound to make me freak out," Eva said. "What on earth have you done?"

Andi smiled at her friend's reaction. She knew Eva wouldn't reject it out of hand.

"Well, it's a small little Christmas party for the Lodge." Best to ease her into the idea.

"Andi, the Lodge doesn't do small parties. Just tell me."

So she did. Andi spilled the story about how Carmen was left in the lurch for an event coordinator and how since she just happened to be there, Andi thought she'd help out.

"But you hate Christmas," Eva said.

Andi looked out the window to the snow-covered pines wrapped with twinkling lights. They were starting to come on as the sun set behind the mountains.

"I did," she said. "I mean, I do."

"Which is it?"

"I might be changing my mind."

"Wow, the Lodge must be working it's magic on you. I didn't think it was possible for you to be converted to the candy cane cause," Eva said. "By the way, how are things? You left a message saying things got screwed up. Did it get sorted out?"

"Ummm, yes," Andi said. She touched a finger to her lips, remembering her kiss with Colin. "Things most definitely got sorted out. I'm actually sharing a villa with this guy—"

"Wait. What?" Her friend managed to get out before being taken over by a coughing fit. After a moment, Eva got herself under control and said, "Sorry, coffee went down the wrong pipe. What do you mean, you're sharing a villa? What on earth is going on?"

"It's really not that big of a deal," Andi said, knowing full well it was a big deal. "There was a mix-up with the reservations, and they didn't have room for me, so Colin offered to share his villa with me, since he was by himself."

"Colin? What do you even know about this guy? How do you know he's not going to murder you in your sleep, or worse?"

"Worse than murder?" Andi laughed.

"It's not funny," Eva said. Andi could picture her friend pacing in their tiny office. If there was something Eva did well, it was worry about things out of her control. "This is serious. You need to get out of there right now."

Andi put the file she was holding down and stood. "Honestly, Eva. He's perfectly safe. He's actually an old friend of Blaine's."

"Blaine? This keeps getting better and better."

"Well, they're not really friends," Andi admitted. "But they did go to school together. I get the feeling there's some kind of history between them. But that's not important. The strangest part is that I've met him before. Remember that trip Blaine and I took to St. Lucia?"

"Vaguely."

"We actually had dinner with Colin on that trip because he was living down there at the time."

"What a coincidence."

"I know, right," Andi said, ignoring the snark in her friend's voice. "Anyway, he's really nice and funny and he's...well, he's kind of cute."

"Wait a minute. Stop everything. Are you saying you like this guy?" Eva's tone shifted.

"I think I do," Andi admitted. "He's been doing what he calls his 'Christmas Conversion' project, showing me how wonderful the holidays can be."

"And it's obviously working," Eva said with a giggle. "Okay, so now I understand what's really going on. What about the fact that he knows Blaine? Isn't that kind of strange?"

"It bugged me at first, but really I don't think it matters. They aren't close, and...well, I can't hold that against him." As she talked, Andi went to the kitchen and poured herself a fresh cup of coffee. "So you'll help me with the ball?"

"You know I will," Eva said. "Tell me what we need to do and I'll be there. But I have to be gone first thing in the morning. My mom has a big dinner planned."

"Thank you. You can stay here—there's an extra room in the villa."

"Perfect, and then you can tell me all about this guy, right?"

Andi swallowed her coffee hard and ignored the question. "After looking at what they have here and what they've done in the last few years, we should be good for decorations, and of course the Lodge will handle the food. We just need to plan a menu. We should be able to utilize the staff to work the party but we still need a theme."

"Okay," Eva said. "I'll work on the theme and then you can tell me about this guy."

There was the sound of the keycard in the lock and Andi

looked over to see Colin, laden with bags, come through the door. She waved her hand in his direction but put her finger to her lips to keep him quiet.

Colin nodded his head and went down the hall to put his packages away. Andi turned her attention back to the phone, and Eva. "I have to go. Call me later."

"Oh, he's there, isn't he? You don't have to tell me now, but you'll tell me sooner or later."

"I'll talk to you later," she said to her friend and hung up before she could hear Eva's protests.

There was no point having her read more into the situation than there was. It was just a kiss. Amazing, and toe curling, sure, but it was still only one kiss. Besides, Colin had made it really clear he didn't want anything more, and as much as Andi would like to pretend she could be the one-night stand type, she wasn't so sure her heart could make the leap. She looked at the tree in the corner of the room. She had to admit, it was beautiful. The lights sparkled, and the fresh piney smell filled her senses. Maybe it wasn't so bad. And Christmas could be a lot of fun this year, if she let it.

"Andi," Colin said, making her jump. She hadn't heard him come into the room.

She turned around and the sight of him made her stomach clench.

"Are you okay?" he asked. "I didn't mean to scare you."

"You didn't," she said. "I was just thinking and..." His slow smile distracted her. Damn. Could he be thinking of their kiss too?

"Andi, I—"

"I should probably get ready," she said, cutting him off. "We have dinner reservations."

Andi did her best to be casual as she walked past him

towards her room, but when her arm brushed his, she knew he could feel the electricity between them just as well as she could.

COLIN KNEW Andi would look amazing dressed in something besides the jeans and sweaters he'd seen her in, but he wasn't prepared for the woman who sat across from him at the restaurant. She was stunning in a simple fitted black dress that showed off all of her assets. But it was her silky dark hair that she'd let loose from her standard ponytail, that mesmerized him. It was shiny and looked so soft that Colin couldn't stop himself from imagining what it would look like splayed across a pillow.

All through their appetizers and steaks, they'd talked about all types of things. She'd seemed impressed with how he'd turned things around in his business, and he'd been equally impressed with her party planning company. She was a driven woman, which only made her more attractive to him, if that was even possible.

Despite the easy conversation between them, Colin couldn't help the feeling that something was holding her back. Andi seemed distracted and distant. He couldn't put his finger on it, but there was definitely something going on.

"Are you up for dessert?" he asked. "The chocolate lava cake looks pretty good." He pointed to the table next to them, trying to distract her out of her thoughts.

"I don't—"

"Come on," he said. "We'll share. How could you pass that up?"

"Honestly, I don't think I can move," Andi said. "I'm so full. That was the most amazing steak I've had in a long time." She leaned back in her chair and when she stretched, her chest pushed out and Colin had to look away. She had no idea the effect she had on him.

Once he had himself under control again, he stood and offered her his hand. "Why don't we walk it off then?"

She accepted with a smile and said, "I think that's a great idea. I could really use some fresh air."

Just feeling her skin against his again made his heart race. They hadn't kissed or even touched since their shared moment by the fire earlier, but now he was like an oversexed teenager. He battled with himself. Part of him—a large part—couldn't wait to get her back to the villa and have the opportunity to show her exactly how she made him feel. But there was something about Andi. He liked her, really liked her. And the more time he spent with her, the more he had to admit to himself that maybe Rose was right. Maybe it was time for him to settle down.

They left the restaurant bundled up in their coats and wordlessly chose the longer path back to the villa. Walking through the woods on the lit path, Colin reached out his hand and took hers.

"I was wondering if I'd scared you away earlier," she said shyly.

Colin stopped short. "Me? Scared me?" He took her other hand and pulled her close. "Oh no, you definitely didn't scare me. Quite the opposite, in fact."

"Is that right?" She grinned and Colin leaned down, touching his lips gently to hers.

He pulled back after only the slightest touch. "That's right," he whispered.

She smiled, but then her face turned serious. "I need to tell you something. But first I need you to answer a question."

Colin's gut reaction was to put his fingers in his ears like a child. He didn't want to hear what she was going to say. Not if he wasn't going to like it. And he had a feeling he wasn't going to like her question or whatever it was she needed to tell him. He swallowed hard and prepared himself to hear the worst. "What's that?"

"I need to know how close you are with Blaine." Colin stopped short. He shouldn't have been surprised; after all, he knew the question would be asked sooner or later. "I mean, I'm pretty sure you aren't going on weekend fishing trips or anything like that," Andi continued. "But, it's important for me to know what's up between you."

Colin dropped one of her hands and ran it through his hair, taking a moment. "Well, since it's important to you," he said after a moment. "The truth is, we used to be close. Really close. In fact, we were like brothers. We lived at each other's houses, and spent all our time together."

"What happened?"

"I stole his girlfriend," Colin said simply. He glanced at Andi to see her reaction but to her credit, she didn't look completely horrified. "We were nineteen, Blaine had moved away for college, and he and Katie were doing the long-distance thing. Trust me, it wasn't planned, and it definitely wasn't my finest moment. But I was young, and our friendship grew into more. I thought she was the one, and Katie told me she loved me and...it was a crappy thing to do. I know."

"It was a crappy thing to do." Colin looked up into Andi's eyes. Instead of the judgment he thought he'd see there, he only saw kindness. "But you were young. That was a long time ago."

"It was," he said. "But these things have a way of sorting themselves out. Remember when I told you that I had a serious girlfriend who cheated on me?"

"Katie?"

Colin nodded. "When Blaine found out, he actually started talking to me again. I'm pretty sure it was only so he could boast about how everything was going so well in his life while mine was falling apart. And ever since, that's been our relationship. Every time we'd run into each other, it's always about how great his life turned out while mine has fallen apart. He's never gotten over it."

"I'm sorry, Colin." Andi squeezed his hand and put her free hand on his arm. "But he's not better than you. His life isn't so great. Not always," she said softly.

Colin flinched. "Does this have something to do with what you need to tell me?"

She nodded and spoke slowly. "It was a very serious relationship. We had our rough spots, but mostly, it was good." She looked down, and kicked at the snow. "But then he left me when I needed him the most." Colin's gut clenched at the sadness in her voice. "It crushed me," she said. "I thought what we had was stronger than that. But I was wrong."

Unexpected anger boiled up in Colin at the thought that Blaine could have hurt Andi so badly. He tried his best to hide his feelings from her so she would keep talking.

"And when it ended, well, I kind of shut down," Andi said. "The only thing left for me was work. So when the holidays came up, I came up here to hide. I couldn't face it." She looked down, and added, "And I can't believe I'm telling you all of this."

"No," Colin said. He squeezed her hands and she met his gaze again. "I'm glad you told me. I could tell there was something on your mind at dinner."

"You could?"

He laughed at her surprise and felt his anger for Blaine diminish. "I know, I can hardly believe it myself," he said. "I'm not generally known for being very perceptive."

"Well, it's been a little while since I've been on a date, and I just thought it was fair that you knew what you were getting in to."

"A date?"

She blushed. At least, Colin thought she did. It might have been the cool air.

"Well, I guess, I thought…never mind."

Was it a date? It'd been so long since he'd gone on an actual date, and not just out for drinks and sex. "No," he said. He leaned forward, letting his lips caress hers again before pulling away. "You're right. It is a date. Our first date."

"Well then, since we agree that it is a date," she said, "I suppose I should tell you that I used to have a rule about dating."

Colin pulled back just enough so they could continue walking, slowly now, towards the villa. "Tell me," he said.

"I know this sounds kind of awkward, but I think I should put it out there because you seem like the type of guy who has different ideas on things."

What the hell did that mean? Instead of asking, he said, "Just say it, Andi."

"I don't sleep with men on the first date."

"And you think I'm the type of man who sleeps with women right away?"

She stopped walking and tipped her head, challenging him with her eyes. "You more or less told me that you don't do relationships, and you're an attractive man, so—"

"You think I'm attractive?" He smiled and she swatted at him.

"Tell me I'm wrong," she said.

Colin shrugged. "I can't." He started walking again.

A few moments later, they reached the front door and Colin slid the key into the lock. Before he opened the door, he turned to Andi, and said, "I might have been that guy before, but I think that might be changing."

"Change is good." She smiled and it was so sexy and

seductive, that it took all the willpower he had not to kiss it away.

He opened the door and waved her in ahead of him. Colin took a deep breath of the crisp mountain air and couldn't help but hope that she was right.

## 9

*T*he cold air blasted through Andi's housecoat and pricked at her skin. Colin was already waiting in the hot tub and steam floated up from the water, creating a mystical cloud around him. It had been her idea to try out the tub since neither of them was ready for bed. And when she saw his hard, naked chest in the water, she was secretly very pleased that he'd agreed to it.

"Jump in," he said.

"It's cold." Andi bounced on her feet and tightened the robe around her.

"I swear," Colin said. "It's beautifully hot in here. Come on."

"Sure, it's good when you're already in."

Colin laughed and splashed some water in her direction. "I'll prove it to you," he said, and before Andi could say anything, he put his hands on the edge of the hot tub and launched himself out of the water.

"What are you doing?"

"I told you I'd prove it to you." Colin flopped into the deep snow next to the deck and started making snow angels with nothing but his wet board shorts on.

"You're crazy," she said, and ran towards him. "Get up before you freeze to death." Andi reached out her arm to him but pulled it back before he could grab it. "I don't think so. You're not going to pull that trick again.

Colin jumped up from the snow and Andi took off running. She untied her robe and let it fall behind her as she leapt into the hot water. Colin was close behind, falling into the hot tub with a loud, clumsy splash.

"Oh," he moaned. "It burns." Colin danced around in the water and Andi was laughing so hard she didn't even bother covering her face from the splashing.

After a moment, Colin relaxed and sank down into the water next to Andi, who was still laughing. "See, I told you it was hot," he said.

"You're ridiculous," she said, when she was finally able to take a breath. "Are you okay?"

Colin wrapped his arms around Andi's waist and pulled her close. His wet chest pressed up against her body fired all her nerve endings and she pulled herself closer so every possible inch of their wet skin was touching.

"I'm just fine now," Colin said. His lips met hers, and maybe it was because of the fact that only scraps of bathing suits were between them, but the sweetness of their earlier kiss was replaced with fire. Andi let her body relax and wrapped one hand around Colin's back. She let her fingers slide over his muscles before squeezing tightly. A sigh escaped her when he moved from her mouth, trailing kisses down her neck. Her body responded to every touch, with bold sensation. But when he reached the swell of her breast, she reluctantly pushed Colin away.

"I'm sorry," he said. He stepped back, putting distance between them. "You did say that you liked to take things slow, didn't you?"

Andi nodded, not trusting herself to speak.

"Well then," he said. "Why don't we have a drink?" Without waiting for an answer, Colin leaned out of the water to a side table, where he produced a bottle of wine and two glasses. He handed her a plastic glass full of red wine. "It might be a little chilled," he said.

Andi took a large swallow. It took everything she had not to throw her glass down and press her body up against him again. It felt good to be close with a man again and with Colin, it felt like she'd known him forever. So maybe it wasn't really breaking her own stupid rule if she slept with him. The thought flew into her mind, but she quickly squashed it. What was she thinking?

"Cheers," Colin said. He held his own glass of wine aloft and waited for her to connect.

She cleared her throat, and said, "To new friends."

"Friends?" He cocked his head.

Andi ignored him, and continued, "And Christmas."

They clinked glasses and took hearty swallows.

"I thought you didn't like Christmas," Colin said when he put his glass down on the edge of the tub. "In fact, wasn't it only a few days ago that you were trying to convince me how much you hated it? Don't tell me my 'Christmas Conversion' plan actually worked?"

Andi laughed. "It did," she admitted. "It's still not my favorite holiday, but I think the company I've had has a lot to do with me enjoying myself this year."

Colin put his hand to his chest in mock surprise. "Who, me?"

She flicked him with water. "Yes, you." Andi slid down, letting the bubbles flow over her and release some of the tension in her shoulders. She tried to keep her mind off the half-naked man sitting across from her and the kiss they'd shared, which left promises of much more to come.

"Can I ask you a question?" Colin asked.

"Why not?"

"Well," he started, "I know you don't think much of Christmas. Or at least you didn't until I came along." Andi looked at him and Colin was predictably smiling. She laughed and took a sip of her wine. "What you didn't tell me," he continued, "was why you didn't like it. I know you mentioned that you wanted to hide, but I get the feeling that there's more to it than just the breakup."

She looked away, up to the stars that filled the night sky. The thought of ruining their perfectly good evening by telling him her story of loss was too much. He'd feel sorry for her if she told him about the baby—everyone did. And then, whatever it was that was happening with them would be gone. No, she couldn't tell him.

"I just don't have a lot of good memories," she said. "And I can't remember ever getting a present that really meant something to me." At least that part was totally true.

"Really?" Colin said. "Even from Blaine? He never got you anything special?"

Andi thought back through the years. Blaine had always leaned towards practical gifts and while she'd always appreciated the cappuccino machine and the bookstore gift certificates, they were definitely not what she'd call memorable.

"No," she said. She drained the last of her wine and Colin leaned forward and refilled her glass without batting an eye at how fast she'd consumed it. "I guess you could say he wasn't too into gifts." Andi took another sip of her drink and set it down on the ledge. "Now, it's your turn to answer a question."

"Anything."

Andi let out a sigh of relief, and asked, "What's wrong with you?"

"Pardon me?" Colin sputtered after choking on his drink.

"Sorry," Andi said and tried to suppress a giggle. "What I

meant was, why are you still single?"

"Oh," Colin said. He put his glass down and moved across from her. He put his hands on her thighs and despite the hot water, shivers thrilled through Andi's body. "I guess because I hadn't met you yet," he said, inching closer to her mouth.

"That's such a line."

"Did it work?" Colin's mouth turned up into a grin.

She struggled to keep her breath even. It was a losing battle. "We should probably get to bed," Andi whispered. "It's a big day tomorrow with the ball and—"

His mouth locked on hers, and not for the first time that night, thoughts of her self-imposed dating rule flashed through her head and almost just as fast, she came up with a dozen reasons why it didn't apply. She pressed her body against his, closing the gap between them. Her drink spilled into the water as Andi reached around Colin's back and pulled him closer. He tasted of the rich wine, and she drank him in.

Andi wrapped her legs around his waist. The feel of his bare, slippery skin on the inside of her thighs caused the pressure to build into a flaming center of molten heat. Colin secured his hands on either side of her legs, letting them slide up and over her bikini bottoms. His fingers teased the ties that secured her bathing suit closed, before plunging them under the fabric to squeeze the flesh beneath.

She pulled her mouth away from his, gulped a breath and let out a moan as Colin moved his mouth to the top of her breast that was just peeking out of the water. She groaned again and tipped her head back, giving him better access to her chest. Colin responded by lifting her up to expose more of her body from the water. With one hand still holding her bottom, his other hand deftly untied her bikini top and swiped it to the side. He grasped her breast and squeezed with just enough pressure to liquefy her resolve.

The cold air bit at her skin, but Andi hardly noticed as Colin's expert hands caressed her, while at the same time his mouth explored her bare skin. The combined sensation built up in her until Andi thought she'd scream out with pleasure. One second before she could do just that, Colin released his grip on her and gently pushed her back to the bench so she was once again covered by the hot water.

"I'm sorry," he said, when he met her gaze.

"Sorry for what?" she breathed. "I wasn't complaining."

"No." He chuckled. "You most certainly were not. But because of your little rule, which I respect," he added quickly, "I think I might be complaining sooner rather than later, if you know what I mean?"

"About that rule—"

"No, no," Colin cut her off. "I respect it. And I respect you and—"

Andi threw herself forward in the water, smashing her chest into his. She met his mouth with a ferocity she wasn't even sure she possessed. Blaine certainly had never brought out the level of want and desire that Colin had ignited in her. She kissed him deep, wrapping her arms around his neck and entwining her fingers in his wet hair. Andi couldn't remember a time when she'd ever been the aggressor in a relationship. Perhaps it wasn't her. It was the man. And this time, the man in front of her was certainly worth the aggression.

"Andi," Colin groaned, pulling himself away from her. "I'm serious. I'm respecting your boundaries. I want to, actually. Although, I must say, you are not making it easy on me."

She didn't let go of him. "I don't believe you," she said.

"Believe what?"

"That you actually want to respect my boundaries, because your body is sure as hell telling me different." She tried to kiss him again, but was stopped when she saw his face and she knew she'd been beat. "Dammit," she said and pushed backwards in the water. She reached behind her and hastily retied her bikini top.

"I've got to admit," he said. "It's really hot to see you so worked up. But I like you, Andi." He started to move closer to her, but she held up a hand to stop him. If she had any hope of cooling down, she needed personal space. "And you might think I'm a sleazy one-night stand kind of—"

"I didn't say that."

"Ah, but you did," he said with a small smile. "But it's not like that with you. I told you I was going to change. And I'm going to prove it."

HE'D PUT HER OFF. Colin couldn't even believe it himself. When she'd said she couldn't or wouldn't have sex with him right away, he was unpredictably okay with it. Of course, that got a lot harder when he saw her in a bikini and harder still when he was kissing her. But he knew it was the right move with her and, instead of feeling frustrated, Colin felt inexplicably happy lying in his bed alone.

He stretched his arms over his head and let out a sigh. Andi made him happy. The last few days were truly some of the best he'd had in a long time. For a moment, he considered climbing out of bed to find her and get one more goodnight kiss. But no, he knew himself too well. He'd shown restraint once; he didn't know if he'd be able to let her walk away again. No, it was definitely a better idea if he stayed put.

Colin reached over to the bedside lamp when there was a knock at the door.

His body responded instantly.

He pulled the comforter higher, covering his boxer shorts.

"Come in."

The door pushed open slowly and Andi stuck her head around the corner. Her hair had been pulled back into a ponytail and gone was the sexy dress and even sexier bikini. Instead she wore her Bugs Bunny t-shirt and fleece pants. Andi had never looked hotter.

"I'm sorry to bug you," she said. She moved slowly into the room. "But I...well...I know this sounds stupid, but I didn't want to be alone."

Colin groaned. "You're killing me, Andi. I told you, I respect your—"

"No," she said quickly. "I don't mean sex." She came closer to the bed and Colin could see the sadness in her eyes.

"Come here." He sat up in the bed and gestured to the space next to him. The mattress sank with her slight weight when she sat and Colin wrapped his arm around her, pulling her close. "Is everything okay?"

She fit perfectly in his arms, and at the moment, he thought holding her was just about the best thing he could think of doing.

"I'm fine," she said. Her voice was muffled against his chest, but she made no motion to move, so he rubbed slow circles on her back. "I was just thinking how nice it's been to be with you. I know it sounds stupid, but for the first time in a long time, I don't feel so lonely."

Colin froze, his hand in the middle of her back. Andi looked up then.

"I'm sorry," she said. "I should go." Andi moved to get up and with one hand, Colin reached up and pulled her gently back down to the bed.

"No," he said, his voice husky. "I want you to stay." He stroked a stray piece of hair off her cheek and looked into her eyes until she blinked and smiled.

"I'd really like that," she said.

Colin slid over, making room for her to crawl under the covers next to him. He couldn't remember the last time he'd ever spent the night with a woman and not had sex with her. Probably because it had never occurred before, let alone with a woman he was so attracted to.

As soon as she tucked her head onto his shoulder, he knew that the night would be a torturous exercise in restraint. In an effort to distract himself, he laughed and said, "I guess men's fantasies about women wearing sexy lingerie to sleep are just that, fantasies." He stroked Andi's shoulder, lifting her t-shirt away from her skin slightly.

"You have a problem with my pajamas?"

"Quite the contrary, actually." He lifted his arm so she could snuggle closer to his chest. When his arm was wrapped securely around her, he added, "In fact, I've never seen sexier nightwear than what you have on right now."

She laughed, but he was serious. Seeing her so relaxed with him at that moment made the old t-shirt and fleece pants hotter than anything else he could have imagined.

He pulled her close and inhaled her sweet scent. She smelled fresh, like the outdoors, and faintly of apples.

"Colin?" She sounded exhausted; her voice was barely a whisper.

"Yes?"

"Thank you," she said.

"Andi, I couldn't think of a better way to spend the night," he said. The weight of her on his chest felt good and he realized he'd meant what he'd said. For the first time in a very long time, Colin felt content. He let his hand slide through her silky hair and kissed the top of her head. "Good night, Andi," he said, but she was already asleep.

## 10

*T*he sound of a phone ringing jarred Andi from her slumber. She rolled over and fumbled around the bedside table before remembering she wasn't in her own room. Had she really spent the night next to Colin? The last thing she remembered before falling asleep was lying in his arms. Before going to his room, she'd crawled into her own empty bed, but the thought of spending the night alone hadn't been an appealing one. Going to Colin felt natural, and he hadn't turned her away.

With her eyes still closed against the morning sun, Andi swept her arms to the other side of the bed. Nothing. Her eyes popped open. She was alone. Except for her cell phone, which was on Colin's pillow. Still ringing.

Andi let out a sigh, stretched her arms over her head one last time and reached for the phone.

"Good morning, Eva.

"I've been trying you for like half an hour. Do you have any idea how much work we have to do today?"

Andi rolled over and looked out the window. The late December sun was just starting to peek over the mountains, sending red and orange rays across the landscape and through the pines. It was the most beautiful thing she could imagine seeing in the morning. Except of course, the sight of Colin, half-naked and wrapped in a towel, which she saw when she turned towards the bathroom door.

"Andi, are you listening to me?" Eva's voice came through the line and Andi realized that she in fact had not been listening.

"Of course," she said.

Colin smiled and mouthed the words, "Good morning."

Like a love-struck teenager, she grinned wide and could feel a blush burn on her cheeks. It was ridiculous. It's not like they had sex. But maybe that was it; sex wouldn't have been anywhere nearly as personal as what they'd shared instead.

"Thank you," she mouthed back to him, pointing to her cell phone.

He shrugged and turned her attention back to Eva. "I'm listening," Andi said to Eva. "But we still need some sort of theme for the party. We might just need to go with a basic Christmas ho, ho, ho theme. You know, wreaths, holly, mistletoe, all that."

"No way. That's way too simple. I have a great idea and I know where we can get some costumes last minute."

"Like, really last minute," Andi said. "You know you need to be here in a few hours."

"Don't you want to hear the idea?"

Andi's eyes tracked Colin's movements across the room to the dresser, where he pulled out a pair of jeans and a clean shirt. She sat up in bed, letting the covers fall to her waist. For one delicious moment, she thought he might drop his towel right in front of her. Instead, he bundled up the clothes, and with a smirk in her direction, made his way back to the bathroom.

"Tell me the idea," Andi said with a small sigh.

"I think we should go with the Night Before Christmas," Eva

announced. "I can get some mouse costumes, and sugar plum fairies. We can even have the staff break into small skits throughout the night. And, wait for it," Eva said. "I found the best soundtrack to play at the end of the night. It's the sound of reindeer hooves and then we get a Santa to call out, 'Merry Christmas to all—'"

"'And to all a good night,'" Andi finished for her. "I'm familiar with it. It sounds great. Let's do it." Andi kept her eyes on the bathroom door, waiting for Colin to reappear. "How did you think of that?"

"Well," Eva paused, "it came to me when I saw that invitation on your desk last night. You know, the one from the Porters."

Andi's stomach clenched the way it always did when she remembered the family she'd once thought of as her own. The same family who'd dropped her the minute their son did.

"Are you okay, Andi? I'm sorry. I really need to learn when to shut up, but I—"

"It's fine," she said and then realized that it, in fact, was fine. The feeling in her stomach was gone as quickly as it came. "I actually kind of forgot all about the party."

"For real? That must be some guy you've got there," Eva said with a laugh. "Well, I guess I'll get to meet him tonight anyway. I'm looking forward to it. Anyone who could convince you that not only is Christmas okay, but inspire you to throw an actual Christmas party, well, he's got to be amazing."

"He is pretty amazing," Andi said with a laugh and then added, "Now stop talking to me and get in the car. We have so much to do."

"Hey," Eva said. "I'm on it. You get out of bed with Mr. Wonderful and get your butt moving."

"I am not in bed with Mr. Wonderful," Andi protested. It was remarkable how well her friend knew her. More often than not, Eva knew her better than she knew herself.

"Whatever. I'm out," Eva said. Andi heard her laughter come through the line before she disconnected.

Tossing her cell to the pillow next to her, she leaned her head back against the headboard and sighed.

"So, I'm Mr. Wonderful, am I?"

Colin's voice spooked her and she sat up sharply to find him standing at the end of the bed with a big smile on his face.

"That was Eva," she said. "She's on her way."

"You didn't answer my question."

"Eva thinks she's funny."

"So, it's just your friend who thinks I'm wonderful? Not you?"

"Stop it." Andi threw a pillow at him, which he caught with one hand. "I have a million things to do." She pushed the quilt off her legs and started to climb out of the bed.

Colin moved around the side of the bed and wrapped his arms around her, pushing her gently back into the mattress. He kissed her soft and sweet on the lips and said, "Well, for what it's worth, I think you're pretty wonderful too."

Andi murmured her appreciation against his mouth and then firmly pushed him off her and to the side. She straddled his waist and planted a quick kiss on Colin's forehead. "Save it," she said. "We have a million things to do."

He smiled a wicked smile and said, "Oh, I can wait. Because tonight will be our second official date."

"I suppose it will be," she said and jumped to her feet. She headed for the door but before she left, she turned back to see him watching her.

"And then there won't be any more excuses," he said.

She opened her mouth before realizing she didn't have any protests. She closed her mouth and blew him a kiss before turning and running down the hall to her own room.

COLIN MOVED QUICKLY through the halls of the main Lodge. Andi had put him in charge of making sure the party room was set up properly and he wanted to be certain that it was perfect. She was really excited about planning the Holly Berry Ball, which felt like a big deal since up until a few days before, she hadn't wanted anything to do with Christmas. Besides, it was a total turn-on to see her in her party planning element.

By the time he got to the banquet room, most of the work had already been done. Buffet tables had been set up in two stations. Andi told him the food would be mostly children's finger food, with a few selections for the parents thrown in. Traditionally, the ball had catered mostly to adults, which she said was ridiculous since the Lodge was filled with families for Christmas. She wanted to make it more fun for the kids. Every time Andi mentioned children, she got a sad, distant look in her eyes. He'd noticed it when they met Kirk and his family at the pond but there was something else going on there too. Something she hadn't told him yet.

Colin wove through the tables and chairs, checking that everything had been positioned according to the hand-drawn plan Andi had given him. There were small stages set up throughout the space that would hold minor performances throughout the night. Everything looked just as it should.

"So, what do you think?" a woman's voice said. Colin turned and saw a tall, striking blonde, with a body to rival any he'd seen on the Caribbean beaches. "You must be Colin," she said, and thrust her hand out.

He took her hand and shook it, realization dawning. "And you must be Eva."

"How did you know?" She put her hands to her chest in mock surprise before laughing.

"How on earth did you get here so fast?" he asked.

"Let me tell you, Colin. When I have somewhere to be, I get there. I like to think that I drive with purpose."

He laughed along with her. She was an easy woman to be around and it wasn't a stretch to see why she was in the party planning business. "Have you seen Andi yet?" he asked. "She sent me to check on the room, but honestly, I don't really know what I'm doing."

Eva started walking and gestured for Colin to follow, which he did. "She has you working already, does she? Well, the room looks great. The staff here are total pros. When Andi told me about organizing the ball last minute, I was worried. But I think with a staff like this, I could pull off any event in only two days. This is amazing. And you should have seen how professional they were when I gave them the costumes."

"Costumes?"

"Andi didn't tell you?" She glanced at him. "It'll be a surprise then." She adjusted chairs as she moved through the room, talking non-stop. "You know, Colin, I don't know what you did to her, but she was dead set against Christmas this year. After everything she's gone through the past few months..." Eva trailed off, shaking her head.

"What do you—"

"Anyway," she cut him off as if he hadn't spoken, "I think she would have skipped the holiday altogether if she could have. But after only a few days with you, she's ready to plan the biggest Christmas party around."

What had Andi gone through in the last year? Colin's mind whirled. She hadn't mentioned anything besides breaking it off with Blaine. Had the breakup been that bad? The anger for his old friend flared up again.

Eva stopped walking and stared at him. "You must be pretty

special." She was smiling, but there was something else behind it. A warning played in her eyes and her voice.

Colin didn't know what to say, so he didn't say anything at all.

"Speaking of Andi." She started talking again, her tone light once more. "I need to find her. I have a million things to go over. Do you have everything under control in here?"

Colin shrugged. "I think I can handle it."

"Good." Eva winked at him and turned to leave. "I'll see you later, Santa."

Santa?

"Wait, what do you mean, Santa?" he called after her, but she'd already left the room.

## 11

"*H*ow about a break?" Eva said, as she opened yet another bag of candy.

Andi wiped her forehead with her wrist and moved to the next bowl. She'd been pouring peppermints into glass vases for twenty minutes, and they still had more to go.

"I don't think we have time for a break," Andi said. "But go ahead. You've been working non-stop for days, plus you drove up here this morning and it's—"

"I meant you," she said. "Besides, we need a Christmas tree. Maybe you can go get one."

"We have a tree, in the lobby."

"And that, my dear, is the problem," Eva said. "The lobby has a tree, but the party doesn't. Now go find that yummy mountain man and get us a tree."

Andi shot her a look that said, *do not bother me with this right now*. Eva ignored it. "Seriously, Andi, he's gorgeous. And he's crazy about you."

"He is not," she protested, but secretly she was hoping for her friend to disagree with her. "Besides, what would make you say that?" Andi turned so Eva couldn't see the smile that took over her face.

"You can drop the act anytime. I'm not falling for it. Besides, anyone can see it." Eva grabbed her arm to spin her around. "I mean really, here it is Christmas Eve and he's in the banquet room with a plan you gave him, ordering around the staff to make sure everything is perfect for you. Of course he's crazy about you. I think he deserves a break, too. Go find him."

Andi grabbed a bag of jujubes and started filling a new vase. "I don't know."

"You don't know about Colin, or about taking a break?"

Andi stopped what she was doing and stared at her friend. "Both."

"No way," Eva said. "That's a cop-out and I'm not going to accept it. Andi, it's been months since Blaine left. You need to get back out there."

"I am out there." Andi picked up a jujube and stuck it in her mouth.

Her friend raised her eyebrow but didn't say anything else for a moment.

"Do we have any more of these?" Andi said with a mouthful. She held up the empty bag and Eva swiped it out of her hand.

"That's enough," she snapped. "Don't insult me by pretending that this guy doesn't mean anything to you. I've known you too long."

Andi risked a glance up at her friend and saw Eva's normally smiling face twisted into a frown. "I...he..." she started.

"Tell me," Eva demanded.

"I don't want to get hurt again." The words came out in a rush. "He's not the relationship type and I thought I could just do a fling. I even tried."

"You tried?"

"I did." Andi sank down into an empty chair. "But at the last minute I came up with this 'no sex on the first date' thing. So we cuddled all night instead."

Eva swallowed back a laugh. "For real?"

Andi shot her a glare. "Well, I used to have that rule. Once." She swallowed hard. "I got scared." She wouldn't look up. Andi knew if she made eye contact with Eva, her friend would know just how scared she really was. It had taken a long time to get over Blaine, or more accurately, his desertion when she needed him.

"Andi." Eva's voice was soft and she crouched in front of her. "You don't have to sign up for forever right now."

"You don't understand," Andi said, finally looking up. "He's not into relationships. He's more or less spelled it out for me."

Hot tears stung at her eyes and she blinked hard to keep them away. She would not cry. Not over a guy she barely knew.

"Here," Eva said. She thrust a bag of chocolate into Andi's lap.

"What's this for?"

"Well, since you're being stupid, you might as well eat yourself into a chocolate coma too."

Eva turned and walked back to the counter and the endless vases that needed to be filled. Andi pushed up from the chair and stalked after her. "What are you talking about? I'm not being stupid."

Eva spun, confronting her. "Oh no? Here you are crying like a little girl instead of taking a look at the facts."

"What facts?"

"Andi," Eva said, struggling to keep her voice even. "This man who you say is a relationshiphobe is currently working his tail off for you and all this after spending the night cuddling with you because you didn't want to have sex. The way I see it, that man is seriously into you and you are being an idiot."

"I am not." Andi knew she sounded childish, but at that

moment she didn't care. She popped a chocolate into her mouth and chewed hard.

"Then prove it." Eva's eyes gleamed with challenge. "Go find Colin and get a Christmas tree."

Andi tossed the bag of chocolates down on the counter. "Fine."

As she left the room, she could hear Eva laughing as she called out, "Just be back in time for the party."

COLIN REFLEXIVELY PUT his arm out to brace Andi as the truck bounced over yet another rut in the road. He hadn't driven in deep snow for years, and the way the truck was working, he was starting to worry that his lack of experience might get them into a little trouble if he wasn't careful.

"Sorry. This road is terrible."

"I'm fine," she said. Andi's hands were gripped on the door as she tried to keep from flying out of her seat. "Are you sure you know where you're going?" She bit her lip like she hadn't wanted to ask the question.

"Are you suggesting that I'm lost?" he teased.

Andi shot him a look before shading her eyes with her hand again. The sun was shining bright overhead, causing a sharp glare on the snow, making it difficult to see. "I wasn't trying to offend you. I know men are touchy about asking for directions. I just thought—"

"It's okay, Andi. I was kidding." He smiled at her and reached over to squeeze her thigh. She'd been distracted and distant since they'd been in the truck. At first, he'd thought she was just nervous about his driving, but the longer they spent together, the more he could sense something was bugging her. "Besides," he said, trying to lighten the mood. "I know exactly where I'm going. Look." He held up a piece of paper with some roughly drawn lines. The guys in the maintenance garage who'd lent him the truck had drawn it for him.

Andi grabbed the paper and stared at it in horror. "Colin, you can't be serious. This is the map?"

He laughed and pointed to the paper. "Don't worry so much," he said. Colin slowed the truck and waited until she met his eyes. "Everything will work out." She blinked hard and looked away.

"I promise." He revved up the engine again. The truck went over a particularly large bump, bouncing Andi towards him on the bench seat. In a quick move, he wrapped his right arm around her shoulders and pulled her close. "I think this is a good spot, don't you?"

He put the truck in park and when she snuggled deeper into his down coat, Colin seriously considered driving again, just so she would stay close. It was probably the party distracting her all afternoon, but whatever it was that had been pulling her away, for the moment at least, it was gone.

Andi didn't say anything, but neither did she make a move to get out of the truck. "Everything alright, Andi?" he asked and kissed the top of her head.

She pulled away slightly and said, "Of course. I was just thinking about how much I was enjoying this right now."

"Me too." He smiled and reached across the distance to put a soft kiss on her lips. "But we better get that tree so we can get to that second date."

"Right," she said. "Let's do this." Andi smiled and licked her lips. It was a subconscious action, but Colin almost grabbed her and had that second date with her right in the cab of the truck.

Instead, he snatched his gloves off the seat, pushed open the door and jumped out of the cab. The snow was deeper than it looked and as soon as they stepped off the packed down track of the road, they sank in, Andi—her legs substantially shorter than Colin's—almost to her knees. Fortunately, they didn't have to go far to find the perfect tree. The forest was thick and they were surrounded by thick, full pines, any of which would make a beautiful tree for the party.

"Have you ever done this before?" she asked Colin.

He walked next to her, trudging through the snow with an ax swung over his shoulder. He glanced at Andi, who looked very sexy in her oversized wool sweater and scarf.

"I remember years ago going with my dad into the woods," he said. "The plan was to chop down the perfect tree to surprise my mom. She always liked the big fir trees that you could buy in the parking lot of the grocery store."

"My parents always got one of those," Andi said. "They were always like a hundred dollars."

"Exactly," Colin said. "So one year, my dad got it in his head to prove to my mom that he could get an equally beautiful tree out of the forest. You have to understand, my mom loved her Christmas trees. It was the most important part of the holiday for her. So it had to be perfect."

"Okay." Andi smiled, encouraging him to go on. "So how did it go?"

"I must have been about eight or nine," he said. "And I remember driving and driving. After what seemed like hours, we got out of the truck and started walking, kind of like we're doing now. My feet were totally numb when Dad finally decided we'd found the perfect spot."

"And you got a great tree?"

"Well, no." Colin laughed. "That's the thing. The place we went had really spindly trees, but instead of admitting defeat, Dad chopped down three trees."

"Three?"

"Yup, then he lashed them all together and tried to pass it off as one, very full pine."

Andi laughed and almost stumbled in the deep snow. Colin caught her easily and steadied her. A jolt went through him at the touch. "What did your mom say?" Her voice came out in a breath. He thought it might be from the hard walking, but he hoped it wasn't.

Colin stopped walking, but didn't let go of her arm. "I think she knew, but she never said anything. Not even when we took it down after Boxing Day. She just looked away and said something about it being the most beautiful tree we'd ever had."

"That's so sweet."

"It was," he said. "I didn't realize it at the time because I was too young, but they were so in love that Dad wanted it to be perfect for her, and she wouldn't wreck that for him. It's one of my favorite memories." He looked into the forest at the trees. He'd never told anyone that story before. Colin looked back at Andi. Why now?

"And now you get to do it again," Andi said softly.

"I do." He leaned down and met her lips with his. Her skin was cold, but her mouth was a warm haven and the kiss heated his entire body. He slid a gloved hand down her cheek and pulled her closer, deepening the kiss.

He could have stood in the forest all day kissing her. But when a cloud moved over the sun, darkening the sky, he reluctantly pulled away. "We should probably hurry."

He spoke the words but didn't make any move to let her go until she stepped back, and said, "We probably should. Besides, there will be lots of time for that later."

His body reacted at her words. But before he could reach for her again, Andi spun around and pointed at a tree. "How about that one? It's perfect."

It was. About eight feet tall, the tree was perfectly filled out.

If the sun had still been shining, Colin would have expected it to glow with Christmas spirit.

"Good choice," he said.

She stepped back and pulled her scarf closer around her face. Without the sun, things were cooling off quickly. The clouds were starting to build and the air held the crisp promise of snow. He'd have to get her back to the warm truck soon.

It only took a few swings of the ax, and the tree came down with a sharp crack that reverberated in the forest.

"I thought you said you didn't have an ax in that bag of yours?" Andi teased as they trudged back through the snow.

"I only bring it out for special occasions," he said. Together they laughed, making the tough work easier. With both of them, they managed to hoist the tree into the back of the truck and secure it.

Before long, they were back on the road and headed towards the Lodge. At least, he hoped they were headed back to the Lodge.

The snow had started to fall as the sky darkened, creating a winter wonderland effect over the forest. It was beautiful, but it worried him a bit too. He wasn't familiar with the area and he had to admit, his map was a little sketchy.

"Are you sure you know the way back?" she asked, as if reading his thoughts. "I swear, I'm not trying to question your manly sense of direction or anything. It's just..."

"What sense of direction?" He laughed and then seeing that she was genuinely concerned, he added, "Don't worry, I promise I know the way back."

It wouldn't do any good to tell her the truth. She had enough on her mind. Besides, Colin thought, the road was starting to look a little bit familiar.

He drove in silence for a few minutes, lost in his thoughts of holidays past. His favorite times were when it snowed heavily the night before Christmas. There was something magical about the snow. He'd set out to experience the perfect traditional festive season, and he'd had it. Colin glanced over at Andi, who was staring out the window at the building storm. He knew it wasn't by chance that the past few days had been so perfect. Whether he wanted to admit it or not, the happiness he felt at that moment had a lot to do with the woman sitting next to him. A whole lot.

"When I was a little boy, I used to love it when it snowed on Christmas Eve," he said, breaking the silence. "There was nothing better than being inside, looking out at the snow, waiting for Santa. It was magical. Like being inside a snow globe." He smiled and looked at Andi.

Kind of like now, he thought, but didn't say, when she slid across the seat and once again snuggled into him.

## 12

*A*ndi wasn't ready for the drive to be over when Colin pulled up in front of the villa to drop her off. With the building snowstorm, she'd secretly been hoping that they'd get lost or stuck, at least for a little while. Being stranded with Colin would have been romantic, but she knew Eva would kill them if they took too much longer; after all, the party was set to start in an hour. But even spending a little bit of time with Colin was just what she'd needed. And watching the sexy way he swung that ax certainly hadn't hurt either.

"I'll see you soon," Colin said and squeezed her shoulder one more time. They'd driven most of the way home with his arm around her, and Andi couldn't remember the last time she'd been so comfortable and so acutely aware of another person all at the same time.

She slipped away from him and put her hand on the door handle. Before opening it, she turned and said, "Thanks for all your hard work today. Don't let Eva steamroll you with anything else."

Colin smiled. Damn, Andi thought, he looked way too sexy when he did that.

"I think I can handle myself," he said.

"You don't know Eva." Andi pushed the truck door open and slid out.

"Andi?" She turned back to see Colin leaning across the bench. "I'll see you later tonight."

His voice held the promise of what exactly later meant and Andi felt her face grow hot with a blush.

"You better get that tree over to the lodge," she said, and closed the door.

Maybe Eva was right, she thought as she walked into the empty villa. Colin definitely hadn't been acting like a guy who wasn't looking for a relationship. Did she dare to think that her escape to the mountains may have turned into something more?

Andi pushed away the thoughts of Colin and what may or may not be happening between them. There was too much to do before the night was over. She'd committed to throwing the best Holly Berry Ball that Castle Mountain Lodge had ever seen, and that was going to require all of her attention. She couldn't allow herself to be distracted by Colin, at least not until the ball was over.

Only moments after she stepped through the doors, her cell phone started chirping. Andi dug it out of her purse to see the screen was flashing, alerting her to missed calls. They must be from Eva, she thought and tossed the phone on the counter. The cell coverage had been spotty in the mountains, and she likely hadn't had any while they were out on their Christmas tree adventure. Eva would have to wait; she was running out of time to get ready.

Andi grabbed the dress Carmen had sent over and moved into the bedroom. There wasn't time to have a shower. She'd have to make do with a quick refresh and a touch of make-up. After slipping into the dress—a fitted red sheath—she turned to check her profile in the mirror. She had to hand it to Carmen; it was a perfect fit. She hoped Colin would like it, or more specifically, the lacy red bra and panties she wore under it. Andi couldn't remember ever being worried about details like that before, but whatever was going to happen with Colin later, she wanted to be prepared. She didn't have time to think about it, though, because a glance at the clock told her she only had thirty minutes until the first guests would start arriving. She needed to get over to the party, fast.

It wasn't until she was ready to walk out the door that Andi thought to grab her phone and check to see what Eva wanted. It wasn't like her to bother Andi with small details. Maybe it was important after all, she thought as she punched in the code for her voicemail.

But it wasn't Eva's melodic voice that came over the line. Instead, it was a voice that made Andi's breath catch in her throat.

AFTER DROPPING ANDI OFF, Colin drove around to the service door by the banquet room and found a few employees on a smoke break who agreed to carry the tree in for him. He was hoping to get back to the villa to get cleaned up himself, but Eva must have had radar because she poked her head outside and spotted him before he could make his escape.

"Colin," she called. He froze, only half in the truck but it was too late to get away. He turned slowly, just in case she was angry that he was late.

"So," she said. "It took you long enough. Did you and Andi have fun?" The glint in her eye told Colin that she was definitely not angry, and likely thought there was a very different reason for their tardiness.

"I'm sorry," he said. "The roads were bad. The guys took the tree in." Colin pointed in the direction where the tree had disappeared.

Eva waved her hand. "It'll be great. But where do you think you're going?"

"I thought I'd go freshen up for the big night."

She laughed and walked through the falling snow towards him. "Oh no, darling. I need you now." Eva grabbed his sleeve and with remarkable strength, pulled him out of the truck and towards the door.

"But the truck..."

"I'll have one of the staff return it. We don't have time. The kids will start arriving soon."

"Kids?"

"Don't you remember? I told you earlier." She flashed him a wicked smile. "And, Andi did say you were great with kids."

Colin's memory flashed back to their meeting earlier. Eva had mentioned something about Santa. He hadn't thought she was serious, though. There was no way she wanted him to play Santa, was there? Colin had envisioned spending some time dancing with Andi, enjoying the ball together and getting a jump on their date.

"Oh," he said. "I don't—"

Eva pushed him through the door and into the banquet room. He let out a low whistle at what he saw. The room had been completely transformed. Things had looked good when he left. But now red, white and green tablecloths were draped over the tables. Jars of candy were on every available surface and large gold and silver stars hung from the ceiling.

"This is..." Colin turned to Eva, who wore a big grin on her face. "It's amazing, Eva. Perfect."

"It is pretty awesome, isn't it? I must admit, when Andi told me about the ball, I had my doubts that we could pull it off. But it turned out perfectly. It's going to be a great night."

"It is," Colin agreed, thinking of his own plans for later that night.

Before he could really get into his daydream, Eva yanked him back to reality. "Come on, I have to get you into the suit."

"So you were serious?"

"Of course I was." She looked at him without a trace of humor on her face. She was serious, alright. "I never joke about Santa."

It didn't take long for Colin to change into the suit Eva had provided him with. He strapped the padded stomach around his waist and rubbed his hands over his round belly. He couldn't help but be impressed with how real it felt. Putting the heavy red coat on over the top, he secured the buttons and turned to admire his profile in the mirror.

Eva had set him up in the staff room. She'd also given him strict instructions to stay in the back room until she came to get him. She didn't want any children spotting him before it was time. The plan was for Colin—or Santa— to sit in the corner of the banquet hall and listen to the kids' last-minute Christmas requests before announcing that it was time for him to get back to the North Pole and start delivering presents.

Then, when Santa was done with his business, Colin planned on finding Andi for a romantic dance or two, as well as maybe a visit under the mistletoe, to kick-start what would be a fantastic second date.

Satisfied that his belly looked jolly enough, Colin secured the beard and finished his look with his wig and hat. He stepped back to examine the finished product. If he hadn't known he was looking at himself in the mirror, he might have thought the actual Santa Claus was standing in the room next to him.

"Ho, ho, ho," he bellowed and held his stomach to see if it jiggled appropriately.

"Not bad," a familiar voice from behind him said. Colin spun and saw a tall, blonde, very well dressed, and very familiar looking man standing in the doorway. "For a minute there, I thought I might have taken a wrong turn and ended up at the North Pole," the man said.

"Bl—" Colin almost greeted his old friend, but something held him back. "Blame it on the decorations," he said in his most Santa-like voice. In an effort to cover his shock, Colin tried to emulate the big guy's bowl of jelly, belly laugh. Might as well stay in character, he thought. At least until he could find Andi and warn her about Blaine. "Are you lost?" Colin asked.

"No," Blaine said. "Well, maybe a little. I'm looking for someone. I was told she'd be back here somewhere. But that's okay, I'll keep looking." He moved to leave but then turned back and said, "Hey, is it too late for a Christmas wish, Santa?"

Colin tugged at his beard and said in his best Santa voice, "Of course not. There's always time for Christmas wishes."

He tried not to cringe. He shouldn't be hiding from Blaine— they had history. But something, maybe that history they shared, or maybe a loyalty to Andi, kept him quiet.

"In that case," Blaine said, "my Christmas wish is for my girl to say yes." He flashed a ring box and Colin caught a glimpse of a large diamond before he tucked the box away. "I'm going to ask her tomorrow morning. Like a Christmas present."

Colin squeezed his hands together to keep from swatting the ring box out of Blaine's hand. He couldn't mean Andi. They'd broken up. And from what Andi had said, it hadn't been a particularly good breakup. But what was Blaine doing here then?

"Ho, ho, ho," Colin said, trying his best to keep his voice light. "Don't you think proposing on Christmas is a bit cheesy?"

Blaine narrowed his eyes, and for a minute Colin thought his cover was blown. "It's not cheesy," Blaine said slowly. "It's romantic and Andi likes that kind of dumb thing. Besides, it's not like it matters. She'll say yes." He ran his hand over his slicked back hair. "But thanks for your opinion, Santa."

He poked Colin in his padded belly but before Colin could react, either to what Blaine had done or said, the other man was gone, leaving Colin to wonder if there was more to Blaine and Andi's relationship than he knew.

## 13

*A*ndi had been hoping to find Colin and sneak in a dance at some point, but the Holly Berry Ball was in full swing, and she hadn't seen him all night. She looked around the room again at all the children running from one candy bowl to the next. Most of them stopped long enough to watch the various performers that Eva had organized around the room. There were sugar plum fairies doing a dance on one stage, while sleeping Christmas mice would wake up, stretch and perform a comedy skit every few minutes; there was even a bed on one stage with Mama in her kerchief and Pop in his cap, settling down for a long winter's nap. Andi was more than impressed. Eva had done an amazing job pulling off the Night Before Christmas theme. It just may have been Party Hearty's finest event yet.

As successful as the party had been, Andi couldn't keep herself from scanning the party room, searching. The voicemail she'd received earlier had thrown her and she was on edge. If she could only find Colin and talk to him, she'd feel better, but he was nowhere to be found. She turned and looked out over the room again. The dance floor had been filled all night with parents dancing with their children, happy kids grooving on their own, and even a few couples enjoying the spirit of the night. A few months ago, heck, even a week ago, if someone had told Andi she'd be at a Christmas party, watching happy families having fun, she wouldn't have believed them. There were a few times when she'd felt the familiar ache and the loss of the child she should have held in her arms, but it didn't linger the way it used to. Instead, thoughts of Colin and the fun she'd had with him took over. Andi didn't want to admit it yet, but her entire attitude towards the holiday may have been forever changed by the presence of one man.

"Well," Eva said, appearing beside her. "What do you think?"

Andi turned to look at her friend. She looked stunning in an emerald green dress, her blonde hair cascading over her shoulders. Impulsively, Andi pulled her into a hug. "It's amazing, Eva. You've totally outdone yourself."

She released her friend, who was smiling from ear to ear. "It is pretty awesome. I think I actually surprised myself," she said.

Andi tried to smile.

"Hey," Eva said. "What's going on?"

"It's nothing really, but, have you seen Blaine?"

Eva choked a little. "Blaine? What on earth would he be doing here?"

"I got a voicemail earlier," Andi said. "He said he missed me, and the girls at the office told him we were here. I think he might have come." Andi scanned the room again.

"Seriously," Eva said. "I don't think even Blaine is stupid enough to show up on Christmas Eve. Don't worry. Just focus on that yummy Colin and—"

"Who's yummy?" Carmen asked, joining the women.

"The gingerbread," Eva answered seamlessly. "I was just saying that the staff here is so easy to work with, I wish we had them all the time."

"Maybe you could," Carmen said. "I need to thank you ladies. This is the best Holly Berry Ball we've had for years. The guests can't stop gushing about it. You both really saved Christmas."

Andi and Eva laughed. "Glad we could help," Andi said, putting thoughts of Blaine out of her head. "Honestly, it was our pleasure."

"Well, I've been talking to our manager and he's pretty impressed too. How would Party Hearty like to host all of our major Castle Mountain Lodge events?"

"Really?" Eva said and then remembered her composure. "Well, I mean, we could see if it fits into our schedule."

All three women laughed and Andi added, "We'd be honored to accept such a generous offer."

"Thank you," Carmen said to her. "It's funny how things worked out, isn't it? Please let me apologize again for the villa mix-up."

"I think that's another thing that worked out," Eva added, with a devilish grin.

Andi could feel herself start to blush, but she didn't care. She looked around again for Colin. "Where is Colin?" she asked Eva. "I haven't seen him all night. He didn't leave, did he?" The thought came to her in a flash and her stomach dropped.

"Settle down," Eva said. "He's here." She laughed and added, "I guess he didn't tell you."

"Tell me what?"

"I needed his help with something."

Andi followed where Eva was pointing and saw Santa, who'd been surrounded by children all night. He was taking turns with the kids, each one sitting on his lap. Andi had noticed a few times that the kids were mesmerized by the jolly old elf and she'd been meaning to ask Eva where she'd found him. She looked back to her friend, realization dawning. "You didn't?" she said.

"Well, you said he liked kids and, well, look at him," Eva said with a grin. "He's clearly a natural."

"The best Santa we've ever had," Carmen added.

Andi felt a surge of pride, which was ridiculous, but she felt her smile grow bigger as she watched him.

"Why don't you go over there and tell Santa what you really want for Christmas?" Eva said and tried not to giggle. "Unless, of course, you've been nau—"

"That's enough," Andi said and swatted her friend on the arm. "Don't you have something you should be doing?"

Andi didn't wait for an answer. She started walking across the room towards Colin. She quickened her pace, the thought of sitting on Santa's lap suddenly more exciting than it'd ever been before.

Miraculously, the crowd of kids started to thin as Andi approached. She couldn't keep the smile off her face. He'd made her so happy and now seeing how good he was with the children, it couldn't be more perfect. She'd worry about what their relationship was, if it was anything, later. For the moment, she was so focused on Colin, that she didn't notice the man who stepped out from beside the buffet tables, until he grabbed her arm and spun her around in mid-stride.

"Merry Christmas, Andi," he said.

It took her a moment to recognize who was standing in front of her, a full few breaths before she realized it was her ex who was holding her by the arm and smiling as if he expected her to be happy to see him. It took her even longer to realize what was happening when he said, "Looks like we're standing under the mistletoe." Blaine wrapped his arms around her, and his mouth met hers in a kiss that was all at once comfortably familiar and completely horrifying.

COLIN HADN'T HAD a chance to recover from his chat with Blaine, let alone have a chance to find Andi to talk to her before Eva had pulled him out to the banquet floor to fulfill his role. With one look at the children, their faces full of magic for the season, Colin knew he wasn't going to be responsible for ruining the Santa fantasy. He'd taken his place on the chair in the corner and ever since, he'd been so busy taking last-minute present requests and listening to children explain away their not so perfect behavior over the last year, that he hadn't been able to focus on Andi. Sure, his thoughts had strayed to her throughout the evening, and he'd seen her walking around, taking charge of the catering staff and making sure every little detail of the night was perfect. She looked amazing in her tight little red dress, and every time she came close, his thoughts definitely strayed to what she might or might not be wearing under that dress.

He was still hoping to have a chance to talk to her about Blaine. If he was going to have a relationship with her, which felt more and more like what he wanted, he was going to have to talk to her, and soon. When he'd looked up from a bossy little girl with red hair and freckles, who had been sitting on his knee for the last five minutes listing her holiday demands, he noticed the group of women standing together, chatting. A moment later, Eva pointed in his direction and Andi's face lit up in a smile.

When she started walking towards him, Colin quickly managed to convince most of the kids who were hovering that they could get an extra piece of dessert if they hurried to the buffet. The thought of Andi sitting on his lap, whispering to him exactly what she wanted for Christmas, was almost too much for him to take. The anticipation grew, building fast. But then, before she could reach him, a man came out of nowhere and grabbed Andi. Colin was halfway out of his Santa seat before he realized it was Blaine.

He spun her around, so Colin couldn't see Andi's reaction and before Colin could take a step, Blaine swept Andi into a passionate kiss. She didn't push him away. Hadn't Blaine told Santa that the engagement was a long time coming?

The air sucked from his lungs and Colin fell back in his chair. A child immediately clambered up on his lap. Colin knew he should put his Santa voice on and get back into the act. There were kids depending on him. He stared at the little blonde girl looking up at him from beneath thick glasses. She blinked once, twice, waiting for him to say something.

He couldn't.

"Santa?" the little girl asked in a small voice. "Are you okay?"

Colin looked up to where Andi had been kissing Blaine. They were gone. Had he imagined it? He looked back to the girl.

"Santa?"

"Ho, ho, ho, sorry about that." Colin gave it his best effort, but he could tell from the girl's face that he hadn't done a very good job. He couldn't focus. His mind spun with thoughts. Where was Andi? Was she still with Blaine?

Colin put his hands to his head, trying to clear his thoughts. They didn't have a relationship, he rationalized. She didn't owe him anything.

"Hi there, sweetie," Eva's voice came from behind him. "You know, I think Santa's getting a little tired and he has a big night ahead of him. Why don't you take this candy cane and I'll help Santa get some rest?"

The little girl gave Colin one more strange, yet concerned look and slid off his lap. She took her candy cane and ran off, no doubt to tell her parents that Santa was having a breakdown. He didn't care. He needed to get out of there. The suit was like a sauna. The beard, suffocating.

Eva grabbed his arm and hauled him from his seat. In a daze, he let her lead her out a side door and into a service corridor. She didn't say a word until they were in the staff room, with the door closed behind them.

"Are you okay?" she asked him as she took off his hat.

"I'm boiling in here," he said, and yanked off his gloves. "I need some water."

She found him a bottle in the fridge, which he chugged while she watched. "I meant, how are you with what happened out there?"

"Is my shift over?" he asked, ignoring the question.

Eva lifted her perfectly groomed eyebrow but didn't push it. "Pretty much," she said, lifting her clipboard. "I just need you to put on your best jolly old elf voice for the microphone in about five minutes. I want to broadcast you saying—"

"Let me guess. 'Merry Christmas to all, and to all a good night'?" He spat out the words.

"You got it," Eva said. "Just try to make it a whole lot jollier. That was pathetic."

Colin yanked at the buttons of his coat. "Excuse me if I'm not feeling so festive right now."

Her face morphed into a mask of concern. "Can I talk to you about that?"

"There's really nothing to talk about."

"What happened out there with Andi," she said. "You are her—"

"We're nothing," he said, his voice laced with bitterness. "She's just staying in my villa. That's all."

"I don't think that's all there is going on," Eva said. Her voice was filled with concern and she tried to take his hand but he pulled back.

"You're right." He paused, glaring at her. "I was hoping there might be a whole lot more going on later, but I guess that's probably off."

Eva recoiled.

He didn't mean to sound so bitter and angry. After all, it wasn't Eva's fault her best friend had been playing him. But with Andi nowhere in sight, likely gone off with her soon-to-be fiancée, she was the closest target.

"That wasn't necessary," she said.

"Wasn't it?" He pulled the jacket off, throwing it to the floor.

"Stop it," Eva said. "Just stop the tough guy act, because you aren't fooling anybody. I can see how much you care about her. I don't care what you say, you have feelings for her."

"Screw you."

"I didn't deserve that," she said.

Colin sat down hard in the seat and hung his head. "No," he admitted in defeat. "You didn't. I'm sorry."

"Look," Eva said. She sat down in the chair across from him. "Just give me five more minutes and then you're off the hook for the night. Go find Andi and talk about what you think you saw. Besides—"

"What I think I saw? I'm pretty sure I know what I saw."

Eva let out a deep sigh. "Just give me five more minutes," she said. "I'll go get the mic. Then you're done." She pushed up from the chair and left the room.

As soon as she was gone, Colin felt bad. She didn't deserve the way he'd treated her. She was here doing a favor for the Lodge, and for Andi.

Andi.

His stomach flipped. Damn her. Eva had touched a nerve with what she'd said. He did care about Andi. Probably more than he should after only a few days. But what had his mother always told him? You couldn't plan on when love would find you; you only had to be open to it. His mother would have loved Andi.

He sighed and rubbed his face hard with both hands. Eva was right about one thing for sure—he needed to talk to her. He quickly stripped out of the rest of the Santa suit and pulled on his jeans and the sweater he'd worn to cut down the tree. He'd hoped to have something nicer to wear, but it would have to do. He wasn't even sure if it would matter anymore.

As promised, Eva was back promptly. He pushed thoughts of Andi out of his head and gave his best Santa performance into the mic. Even to his own ears, it sounded pretty good. Colin could imagine all the kids in the banquet hall getting excited and their parents shepherding them off to bed. He actually smiled when he clicked it off and handed it back to her.

"Thank you," Eva said. "You did great. And now you're done." She smiled warmly and turned for the door. Before she left, she turned back, and said, "Colin?"

He looked up from the table.

"Go talk to her," she said. "Before you make a decision you'll regret, go find her."

## 14

*A*ndi handed out goody bags to smiling, excited children and did her best to smile and say Merry Christmas to each of them. Just because her life was spinning out of control didn't mean she couldn't be professional. She tried not to think of Blaine, who she hoped was behaving himself in the lounge where she'd sent him. Her thoughts kept returning to Colin.

She needed to explain things to him. He must have seen Blaine. And the kiss. What could he be thinking? But maybe Colin didn't care. After all, it wasn't like they were dating, and despite the connection she'd had with him, Colin wasn't into relationships. Her chest ached at the idea that Colin might not view their time together the way she had. It didn't matter, she told herself.

But it did matter. It mattered a lot.

She couldn't think about it yet. For the moment, she still had a party to run. One of the elves had fallen ill, so Andi jumped in to hand out the goody bags. It was a mindless job, which left her brain free to replay what had taken place.

.   .   .

WHO DID Blaine think he was, kissing her like that? She would have smacked him across the face if she hadn't been standing in a room full of children. And with Carmen, who'd just hired them and likely witnessing the whole thing, there was no way she could react the way she wanted to.

As soon as Andi could detach herself from his grasp, she'd dragged Blaine out of the banquet room and into the kitchen. She'd managed to keep herself under control until the doors closed behind them.

"What is wrong with you?" she said, releasing his arm. "Why are you even here?"

"I missed you."

"You have no right to kiss me like that." Andi struggled to keep her voice even. It didn't work.

"I'm sorry," he said. He didn't look sorry though. He looked smug and arrogant. Had he always looked that way and she just hadn't noticed?

"Why are you here?"

He took a step towards her, so Andi instinctively took a step backwards and crossed her arms in front of her chest.

"I missed you," he said again. Blaine reached out and stroked her face with the back of his hand. Shivers ran through her body and she had to fight the urge to wipe his touch off her skin. "You weren't at the party last night and I realized how much I missed you. I called your office and they told me you were here."

"Of course I wasn't at your party," she said. "You couldn't have really expected me to be there. Not after everything."

"Andi, I screwed up."

"Yes, you did."

"Can I—"

"You need to go," she said. "I have work to do."

"I came all this way," he said. "It's Christmas Eve."

"And?"

"It's a blizzard out there. I can't drive back tonight."

"You can't stay here." Andi's thoughts flew to Colin. They were supposed to have their second date. Would he still want to?

"Look," he said. His voice took on the same suave tone he used to use to get what he wanted. "I'll go have a drink and we can talk later."

Andi had been about to protest when Carmen had found her and told her they needed help with the goody bags.

"Fine," she said. "I have to go."


COLIN'S VOICE over the intercom brought Andi back to the present. She couldn't help but smile while he delivered his exiting lines as Santa. He really had done an excellent job.

"Are there any more bags?" A lady with three children stood in front of her, forcing Andi to focus.

"Of course," she said. "Here you go." She handed each of the kids a goody bag. "Did you have fun?"

They nodded and assured her they did and then they were gone. After Santa's announcement, the party had definitely started winding down as parents were in a hurry to get their children off to bed. Andi was so busy saying good night to satiated partygoers and handing out bags that she didn't notice when Colin joined the line. She handed him a bag without looking up.

"I'd rather talk to you," he said. "If you have a minute."

Her body thrilled at his voice. She looked up. His face was hard. He'd seen the kiss.

"Colin," she said in a voice she didn't recognize as her own.

"Can you get away?" He gestured to the bags and the now dwindling line.

Andi nodded. "Come on," she said.

They walked together, not touching, but close enough that she could smell the scent of pine that still clung to his sweater.

When they reached a bench far enough away from the party for it to be quiet, Andi sat. All at once she was exhausted from the craziness of the whole evening.

"So," he said. "Am I correct in assuming our date is off?"

"I don't want it to be," she said.

"How do you think Blaine will like that?" He was so cold and different from the Colin she'd gotten to know that Andi sat back, putting distance between them.

"You know I'm not with Blaine."

"Really? Because from the looks of it, you're still very much together." He bit out the words.

That did it. Andi sat up straight and looked Colin in the eyes. She was done sitting by, listening to him act like a wounded little boy. Especially since he didn't even want to be with her. At least not for longer than one night. And two could play at that. "What do you care?" she shot back.

"Pardon?"

"I asked you why you care," she said, satisfied by his shocked expression. "You said yourself that you're not a relationship kinda guy, so what business is it of yours if another man kisses me?"

"I just—" he started to say, and then paused. "Well, I guess it isn't."

"No, it's not." She sat back and crossed her arms. What had he been about to say?

They sat in strained silence for a minute before Colin spoke again. "Look, Andi," he said. She turned to look at him. His face had lost its hard lines and he looked sad, almost regretful. "I'm sorry if I was an ass. But I really don't want to have anything to do with stealing another girl from Blaine. I shouldn't have ever... well, I just shouldn't have."

Andi's head spun. What did he mean—dating? She took a breath and let her arms fall to her sides. Her hand brushed Colin's, the touch of his skin sending a rush of heat through her. "Colin, I told you. I'm not Blaine's girlfriend," she said.

Colin raised his eyebrows in question.

"I'm not."

"Excuse me if I have trouble with that. You looked pretty cozy out there. And from what he said—"

"You spoke to him?"

Colin shrugged. "He thought he was talking to Santa. It doesn't matter."

"It does." She glared at him, but then softened, and said, "The truth is, we dated. You know that." She waited for a moment and when he didn't say anything, she continued, "It was serious. You know that too. But it's over. It's been over for a long time. I have no idea what he's doing here."

"And it's really over?"

Andi's thoughts flashed from the man she used to think she loved to the one sitting in front of her. There was still so much she wanted to know about Colin, but there was no doubt in her mind that, even after a short time, there was definitely love between them. At least on her end. And it was very different than any she'd felt before. Even if it was for just one night, she thought, she'd chance it. "It's definitely over." She took a chance and slid closer to him so their knees were touching.

For a moment, he didn't say anything and Andi was afraid she'd pushed too far. He opened his mouth to say something, but before he could, she reached forward, put her hands on either side of his face and crushed her lips to his.

Her kiss was hot and hungry. His stubble scratched against her palms. She inhaled deeply, taking in his scent of perspiration and pine. She pulled him closer, working his lips until he matched her passion with his own. Colin's hand slid behind her and his fingers dug possessively into her back. All at once, they couldn't get close enough. She pressed up against him as best she could from their sitting positions. Andi heard a moan. Was it her? Or did the sound come from Colin? She couldn't be sure, and she didn't care.

When she finally pulled away, Andi took a deep breath before opening her eyes. Had he understood? Not only was there nothing left between her and Blaine, there was so much between them. Maybe too much. Slowly, she opened her eyes. He was watching her, a small smile on his face.

"So," he said. "Are we still on for that date?"

AFTER THAT KISS, Colin couldn't get Andi out of there fast enough. He knew Blaine must still be around somewhere, but he couldn't bring himself to care. Despite the fact that they used to be good buddies, Colin couldn't help but feel protective towards Andi. Blaine was responsible for breaking Andi's heart, and for that reason alone, Colin knew he would never be friends with Blaine again. Never mind the fact that he had very strong feelings for Andi. But there'd be time to figure things out with Blaine later. First, he needed to get Andi alone and see what was behind that kiss. She had kissed him with more passion and heat than he'd ever experienced before. And you couldn't fake a kiss like that.

They hurried down the hall back to the banquet room, where the party was dying down. Despite his hurry to get started on their date, Andi still had to touch base with Eva. Colin glanced over at her walking next to him. She was gorgeous in her red dress. Her skin was flushed a very appealing shade of pink, likely from their kiss. He wanted to reach over and take her hand, but he didn't trust himself to touch her again. Not until they were alone, anyway. He didn't plan on letting go the next time.

Colin waited on the edge of the room while Andi chatted with Eva. After a moment, she turned and waved Colin over.

"I'm going to give my key to Eva," she said when he got close enough. "She'll have to stay in the extra room, if that's okay with you?"

"Of course it's okay," Colin said. He smiled apologetically at Eva. Hopefully she'd forgiven him for acting like a jerk.

"That's a damn good thing," Eva said. "Because there aren't any rooms left and there's no way I'm sleeping in the lobby."

"It's turning out to be a really good thing that I have a whole villa," Colin said, and then turned to Andi. "Are you almost ready to get going?"

She smiled a smile he knew was meant just for him. He had to fight the urge to kiss her right there in front of Eva. Andi turned to her friend and said, "You'll take care of...what we talked about?"

"I'll do my best." Eva nodded.

Colin glanced between the two women, and then decided he didn't want to know the details of what they were talking about.

"I'm ready, if you are," Andi said. Together they turned to leave and at the same time, froze. Blaine stood in the doorway of the banquet room. Colin's skin bristled and he fought the urge to put his arm around Andi. To lay claim to her. But the truth was, he wasn't sure that he held any claim over her at all.

"Damn," Andi whispered. "I'm sorry, Colin," she said to him. "I think I'm going to have to deal with this."

Spotting them, Blaine walked over. His eyes were full of questions as he glanced between them all. "Colin?" He looked between Eva, Andi, and Colin, searching their faces. Finally, Blaine reached out and pulled Colin into a manly hug. "I didn't know you were back from the islands. What are you doing here?"

"Hey," Colin said, extracting himself from Blaine's awkward embrace. He took a step back, closer to Andi. "I got back only about a week ago. Just in time for the holidays."

Blaine's gaze flicked back to the girls. "Are you and Eva...you are, aren't you?" He wiggled his eyebrows in a suggestive way that made Colin want to punch him. "It's a small world. Who would've thought it?" Blaine said. "You and Eva."

Before anyone could dispute Blaine's assumption, Andi said, "Blaine, you have to go."

"Baby, we need to talk." He reached out and grabbed Andi's arms.

Colin fought back a growl and clenched his fists together to keep from grabbing his hands away from Andi.

Andi shot a quick glance to Colin before answering him. "Tonight's really not good, Blaine. It's been a long day and I have plans."

"What plans could you possibly have on Christmas Eve?" he said. Colin wasn't surprised. Blaine was a man used to getting what he wanted.

"No," she said. "I'm not doing this right now."

"Tomorrow then?"

"Tomorrow's Christmas."

"I can't think of a more perfect time to talk about us," Blaine said, and Colin's memory flashed to the ring he knew Blaine had. The ring intended for Andi.

Andi let out a deep sigh and shook her hands free from Blaine's grasp. "Go home, Blaine," she said. "If you really want to talk, we'll do it when I get back to the city."

Blaine's faced twisted with a mixture of shock and anger. Colin crossed his arms over his chest and tried to keep the smug look off his face.

"Home?" Blaine asked incredulously. "It's almost eleven o'clock on Christmas Eve and you want me to go home? In a blizzard, no less."

"Blaine—"

"No," he cut her off, his tone changing again. "I'll just get a room and we'll talk in the morning. Christmas in the mountains will be very romantic."

Before either of them could say anything, Eva stepped forward and said, "There are no more rooms. They're overbooked as it is." She looked pointedly at Colin and Andi.

"What am I supposed to do?" Blaine asked.

"Maybe you should have thought about that before you came," Eva shot back.

"Eva." Andi held her hand up.

Interesting, Colin thought. Even her best friend didn't like her ex. Not that it was a surprise; thinking back, not many people did like Blaine. He was an arrogant ass, even in high school.

"Sorry," Eva said. "The best they can do is offer you a couch in staff residence and a voucher for another time. Which they don't really have to do, since you didn't make a reservation," she added.

"Staff residence?" Blaine's voice raised a level. "You have to be kidding me." Then he turned to Andi, who was looking more and more exhausted as the exchange went on. "I'll just stay with you," he said.

"Well, I don't exactly have a—"

"She's staying with me," Colin interjected.

"Oh," Blaine said, looking between them. "Are you all staying together then?" Confusion lined his face as he looked between the three of them again.

"We are," Andi said. "Colin was nice enough to offer me the use of his spare room when the Lodge lost my reservation.

Because it's Christmas and all. Eva's staying, too, because she came up tonight to help out with the ball."

"So, you're not together?" Blaine waved his finger between Colin and Eva.

"No," Colin said. "I just happened to be here at the right time."

"How convenient." Blaine narrowed his eyes at him. "Well, since you're being such a Good Samaritan, old friend, you won't mind letting me crash, too, then. You know, since it's Christmas and all." Blaine was a smart man, and Colin had no doubt from the other man's reactions that he had quickly figured out that something else was going on.

Colin clenched his hands into fists. The smug smile on Blaine's face grated on him, and he had to restrain himself from physically removing Blaine from the Lodge himself. It was taking all of his self-control to behave.

"Unfortunately, I'm all out of rooms," Colin said. "Looks like you're headed to the staff residence, or maybe there's an empty couch in the lobby?"

"I don't think so, buddy." Blaine emphasized the last word. He squared up in front of Colin.

"And what exactly would you like to do about that?" Colin knew he was being a jackass, but he couldn't help it.

"I see what's going on here," Blaine said, his voice full of bitterness. "It's just like old times, hey, Colin?"

Colin's entire body tensed and he might have taken a swing at Blaine if it hadn't been for Andi's hand on his arm.

"Colin," she said softly. "Don't do this."

He looked in her eyes, and let his body relax.

"We can't let him sleep in the lobby," she said.

"Sure we can," Eva chimed in.

"Colin," Andi said, ignoring her friend. "It's Christmas."

Colin looked around the small group. Eva shook her head

and stuck her nose in the air. He skimmed over Blaine, who was looking pompous and sure of himself. Colin's gaze landed on Andi. She didn't look very happy with the way the evening was turning out either. He could barely remember the closeness they'd shared earlier in the woods; it seemed so long ago. Her kiss still lingered on his lips, but the promise of another was fleeting.

Colin swallowed hard, knowing he would regret his decision. He didn't take his eyes off Andi when he said, "It is Christmas. I'm sure we can find room."

# 15

*A*ndi woke with an elbow to her ribs. Her eyes popped open and she stared directly into a mass of blonde hair on the pillow next to her. She'd forgotten how awful sharing a bed with her best friend was. Andi was convinced Eva's wild sleep patterns were the reason her friend was still single. Any man would wake up black and blue after sharing a bed with her.

She looked at the bedside clock. Seven. Andi groaned and rolled over. Maybe if she slept all day, she wouldn't have to deal with Blaine. Or Colin. She knew it couldn't have been easy for him to offer the extra room to Blaine. Lord knows it wasn't easy for her either, but even she knew it was the right thing to do. Andi flipped to her back and stared at the ceiling. How did everything get so messed up?

"Are you done?" Eva asked, her voice thick with sleep and annoyance.

"Done what?"

"Tossing and turning," Eva said. She flipped over so she was staring at Andi. "I swear, I don't know how anyone can sleep with all your thrashing."

"My thrashing? Right." Andi returned her gaze to the ceiling.

"Merry Christmas?"

Andi rolled over to her side. "What a mess. I don't suppose you'd get rid of him for me, would you?"

"Blaine, I presume?" She laughed. "You probably want to keep the other one, right? Or at least you certainly did yesterday."

"I don't know what I want anymore." Andi hugged a pillow to her chest. "It doesn't seem so simple anymore."

"Was it ever?" Her laughter stopped, and Eva's voice softened. "Andi, you don't do simple. I've been trying to convince you for years, but even I know you aren't built for flings. That's okay." She paused. "Heck, it's better than okay. I could probably learn a few things from you."

"Because I've been so successful in love." Andi rolled her eyes.

"You have." Eva sat up in bed, jerking the covers with her. "I may not like Blaine, and it's no secret that he's totally not right for you, but you still had something special with him. I consider that a success. But what I consider an even bigger success is that you learned from it and you're still willing to try again. And now look at you. There is a very handsome man out there who is totally diggin' you. I consider that a monumental success."

"I told you yesterday, he's not into relationships. And I tried to be casual, Eva. I really did. But you're right. I'm just not wired that way."

Eva slipped out of the bed, tossing the covers over Andi's head. "Well, the way I see it, you're not going to know either way until we get out there. Now come on. I need some coffee, and with any luck there'll be some Baileys in it."

AFTER A QUICK SHOWER, Colin was ready to face whatever

craziness was going to be waiting in the living room. Maybe Blaine would have figured out he wasn't welcome and would be long gone. But somehow, he didn't think that was very likely.

Sure enough, when he walked into the room, he was greeted by Blaine, who, much to his dismay, had not only not left for the city, but had also made himself quite at home.

"Morning," Colin muttered in Blaine's direction and moved into the kitchen area to grab a cup of coffee. "Roads clear yet?"

"Not sure," Blaine said. "I haven't checked. What's the rush, right? It's Christmas, after all."

Colin turned and said, "Look—"

He stopped, distracted by the sight of Eva and Andi coming down the hall into the living room.

Before he could put down his mug, Blaine was already across the room, trying to pull Andi into a hug. "Merry Christmas," he called. The man behaved as if this were a normal holiday morning instead of some twisted facade. Colin smiled a satisfied smirk when Andi pulled away from his attempt at a kiss, just in time for his lips to land on her cheek. She twisted out of Blaine's embrace and looked in Colin's direction.

"Merry Christmas, Colin." Her voice was quiet, but her eyes connected with his and a glimmer of hope sparked deep inside him. Maybe the day wouldn't be a total loss. He moved towards her, ready to take her into his arms. Spending the night without her next to him, he'd been acutely aware that something was missing. She filled a space he hadn't even realized was empty.

"Did you sleep well?" he asked when he was only inches from her.

She nodded but he knew she was lying because she looked down and would no longer meet his eyes.

"And what am I, the Grinch?" Eva's voice came from beside him. He'd forgotten she was there. "Merry Christmas, guys." She laughed and Colin turned to give her a hug.

"Sorry," he said.

"Oh, that's okay," Eva whispered into his ear. "I know I'm not your Christmas wish right now."

She pulled away and gave him a wink. "Okay, okay. That's enough of the schmaltzy stuff. Why does everyone get all sappy on Christmas morning anyway? Let's have some coffee and Baileys."

Andi laughed. "You know what? I actually think that's a great idea."

After they all had a coffee in their hands and were seated in the living room around the tree, songs playing in the background, Eva looked at Blaine and asked point blank, "So when are you headed back down the mountain?"

"I thought I'd stay today," he said.

Andi choked on her coffee. "I don't think—"

"It's Christmas, after all," he said as if Andi hadn't spoken. "Andi shouldn't have to spend it alone."

"She's not alone," Eva and Colin said at the same time.

Blaine looked at each of them in turn. "Don't you have some family thing today?" he asked Eva.

Eva nodded. "Yes, but—"

"Like I said, Andi, you shouldn't be alone." He shot Colin a pointed look.

Colin squeezed his hands in a fist. What the hell did Blaine think he was playing at? He'd done his charitable holiday deed; he'd given him a bed for the night. But he was just about done with their little high school reunion.

"I think you should go home," Andi said to Blaine, with a quick glance to Colin. "We can talk when I get back."

Ignoring her again, Blaine jumped out of his seat. "I brought something," he said. "I think we should all have some." He disappeared into the kitchen, returning a moment later clutching four glasses in one hand and a bottle of champagne in the other.

"Champagne? In the morning?" Colin asked.

"Do you need some orange juice in yours?" Blaine retorted. "You always were a lightweight." He popped the cork, letting the froth spill over the top. He poured and handed the glasses around, oblivious of Colin's building rage and the growing discomfort in the room. When he was done, he said, "Before I make a toast, there's one more thing."

Damn! The ring. Colin had forgotten all about it. Or more likely, blocked it from his memory. He stood up from the couch ready to...do what? He didn't know. Before he could think of anything to do or say, Blaine had dropped to one knee and was pulling out the box.

"You have to be kidding?" Colin heard Eva say.

It was too late. Colin froze and fixed his gaze on Andi, whose face had taken on an unnatural shade of white.

"Blaine, what are you doing?" Andi managed to say.

Blaine didn't appear to hear her, or more likely, didn't want to, because he launched into what must have been a prepared speech. "Andi," he said. "The other night at my family's party, the one we always attended together, I looked around and realized something. I realized I needed you by my side. I missed you."

He just realized it? Colin thought.

"I missed the way we were together," Blaine continued. "We were good together. And yes, we had a few rough patches, but we should have stayed and fought it out. We gave up too easily. And, I think it's time we did this thing properly. Andi Williams, will you marry me?"

That was his idea of a proposal? Colin almost laughed at the absurdity of it. Blaine obviously didn't even realize what an amazing woman he was proposing to. A woman who deserved a hell of a lot more than some canned speech.

The room was silent. Andi hadn't moved. She looked like she might throw up. Every fiber in his body wanted to go to her. But he knew he couldn't. It wasn't his situation to fix and he needed to see her reaction, just as much as Blaine did. Maybe more. After what felt like an eternity, Andi let out a slow breath. "Blaine, I—"

"You don't have to answer right away," Blaine said. He hopped up from the floor and pressed the ring box into her hand. "Think about it. Think about how great we could be. And now," he said to the room, "a toast." He raised his glass. "To Christmas and the power of love."

In turn, everyone mechanically raised their glass, muttered something, and they all clinked at the farce of what had happened. Without drinking, Colin put the glass down. She hadn't said yes, yet Blaine was behaving as if she had. It was typical for Blaine. But Andi also hadn't said no, either. And for the first time since the drama had started, he tore his gaze away from Andi and stared out the window.

She didn't say no, a voice in his head repeated.

From somewhere behind him, he heard Eva say, "I'm sorry, Andi. I really, really don't want to leave right now, but I should get going."

"So soon?" Blaine asked. "Things are just getting started." Colin cringed and his shoulders tensed.

"Goodbye, Colin. Thank you for your hospitality," Eva said. Still, Colin didn't turn around. He raised his hand in acknowledgement and continued to look out the window at the snow-covered trees.

She didn't say no, he thought again. Which meant he'd lost his chance.

ANDI STOOD at the door for a few seconds after Eva left. She wasn't sure how she was going to face the mess in the living room alone, but she understood that Eva had to go. Besides, it was her mess to clean up. And it shouldn't be so hard. Should it? After a moment, she took a deep breath and returned to the living room, determined to put an end to the madness of the morning.

"I'm going to make breakfast," Blaine announced.

Andi was about to protest, when she noticed Colin still standing at the window. She went to him.

"He seems to be making himself at home," Colin said, without looking away from the window.

"I'm sorry, Colin," Andi said.

"For what?" He turned then. His face was an unreadable mask. "Congratulations."

"No," she said. "It's not..."

He moved past her and sat on the couch.

"Colin," she said. She sat down next to him. "Don't."

"It's okay," he said. His face didn't give anything away and she wanted to reach for him but she stopped herself. The closeness they'd shared only a day before seemed very far away. "You two obviously have unfinished business."

Unwanted and totally unexpected tears sprang up in the corners of her eyes. She'd known Christmas was going to be awful this year, but nothing could've prepared her for experiencing her first marriage proposal from a man who had broken her heart, while another man, one she shared an undeniable attraction with, stood by and watched.

"No," she said. "We don't. I told you, it's over between us."

"Andi," Colin said softly. "You didn't say no."

A tear broke free and slid down her cheek. No, she hadn't.

Was there a part of her that still wanted Blaine? That wanted the comfortable, successful life he represented? The family they almost had? She glanced behind her to the kitchen, and then back to Colin.

"Hey," Colin said. "Don't cry." He reached out and with a touch so gentle she had to close her eyes, he wiped her tears away. His fingers lingered on her cheek. Andi held her breath, ready for the kiss she was sure would follow. She longed for the taste of him on her lips again. She leaned forward, ready.

He released her and Andi opened her eyes. "I have something for you," he said. "A present."

She swallowed her disappointment. "You do?"

"Well, it is Christmas, after all." He rose from the couch and went to the tree. There was a box wrapped in red paper that she hadn't noticed before. It had a simple green bow on it. He handed it to her, and said, "It isn't much. But when I saw it, I thought of you."

She looked up from the box, into his eyes. "I don't know what to say."

He tried to laugh. "You haven't opened it yet. Go ahead."

Colin walked over to the window and looked out again, so she carefully tore at the paper.

Andi looked down at the present and carefully worked her fingers under the wrapping. She exposed the box and lifted the lid. Inside, nestled carefully in paper, was a snow globe. She lifted it out of the box and let out a gasp. It was a winter scene of a frozen pond encircled by pine trees. On the pond, a tiny couple skated hand in hand. She turned the crank and "Winter Wonderland" played from the tiny speaker. When she shook it, snow fell lightly over the pair. It was perfect.

"Colin," she breathed.

"I told you, it isn't much," he said without turning around.

"This is the most beautiful gift I've ever received."

He shrugged and turned around. "I wanted you to have something to remember your holiday by. You know, the Christmas you didn't want. I know it's not a ring or anything, but I was kind of hoping...well..."

"Thank you," she said through a veil of tears.

She rose from the couch, put the globe down on the table and crossed the room in two steps. "Thank you," she said again and took his face in her hands. His morning scruff scratched her skin and she leaned forward to meet his lips. He tasted deliciously like coffee. She pulled him closer. The need to feel him against every part of her body was stronger than she could bear.

"WHAT THE HELL?" Colin heard Blaine's voice from far away.

He tightened his grip on Andi, slid one hand down her back and deepened the kiss. He had her in his arms again; he wasn't going to let go. Listening to the low moan come from her throat, it was clear that he no longer needed to worry.

"I said, what the hell?" Blaine's voice again.

Before Colin could react, Andi was ripped out of his arms and Blaine shoved her behind him, pulling the tough guy protector act. Only Andi didn't need to be protected.

"Blaine, what are you doing?" Andi demanded. She reached for Colin, but Blaine blocked her.

He turned his back to Andi and spoke to Colin. "What do you think you're doing, kissing my fiancée?"

"I'm not your—"

"Blaine, I think we—"

"Keep your hands off her, asshole," Blaine said. "Still can't get your own women, hey? You need to steal mine."

"Blaine, it's not like that," Colin said.

"Really? Because that's exactly what it looks like. And remember how well that turned out for you."

Colin flinched, but wouldn't back down. "I think you need to calm—"

"History's repeating itself, isn't it, old friend?" Blaine glared at him. "You should go."

"You do realize this is my place?" Colin stood tall. If Blaine wanted a fight, he'd give him one.

"Blaine," Andi said. "That's enough."

He ignored her and spoke again to Colin. "If you ever touch my fiancée again, I'll—"

"I'm not your fiancée," Andi yelled.

Colin smirked and Blaine whirled around to stare at her. "What did you say?"

"I said, I'm not your fiancée." Andi's voice had calmed, but her whole body vibrated. It wasn't hard to see that she was barely containing her rage. "I didn't say yes and you didn't give me a chance to say no. But it's no, Blaine. I will not marry you."

"Is this because of the baby?"

Baby? Colin felt the air leave his lungs all at once. "You have a baby?" he asked the question, but nobody heard.

Over Blaine's shoulder, he saw the look of hurt flash on Andi's face and her hand fluttered to her stomach before dropping to her side again.

"I shouldn't have left," Blaine said, his voice softer. "When everything happened, when we lost her—"

"Don't," Andi said.

"Andi, I panicked," Blaine continued. "I didn't know what to do. I'm sorry. It was hard on me too, but we can try again." He grabbed for her hand, but she pulled away. "Andi, we can be that family you've always wanted." His voice held an edge of desperation.

Colin's mind spun. Andi had said Blaine had left her when she needed him the most. But she hadn't mentioned why. Not that there'd been a chance for her to tell him. But it all clicked into place. Her reluctance to celebrate Christmas. The pain in her eyes when they'd been with Sarah and Kirk and their children. No wonder the holiday was so hard for her. But he'd helped change that for her. He knew he had. He locked his gaze on her. Waiting.

"No," Andi said to Blaine. She shook her head slowly. Colin could see the pain in her eyes when she said, "No. I don't want that." She looked up and met Colin's eyes. "

Colin smiled and hoped his smile conveyed to her everything he needed it to.

She turned back to Blaine and said again, "I don't want that now, not with you."

"But, Andi—"

"No, Blaine." She went to the table and retrieved the ring box. Andi pressed it into his hand. "It's over. We're over."

Colin stepped around Blaine and stood next to Andi. He didn't take her hand, but stood close enough to feel the heat from her body. "You heard her," he said to Blaine. "I think it's time for you to go."

Blaine looked between the two of them. "So this is how it is," he said. "You think he can give you what you want? And you," he said to Colin. "Still picking up my leftovers."

Never in his life did Colin want to hit another man more than at that moment. But Andi put her hand on his arm, stilling him. He could feel her shaking, but she very calmly looked at Blaine and said, "Please leave."

Blaine glared at each of them and without another word he turned and went down the hall. Moments later, he reappeared with his bag in hand. "I won't ask again," he said to Andi. "If I walk out that door, it's over."

Andi slipped her hand in Colin's. "I'm counting on it," she said calmly.

Colin squeezed her hand but kept his face blank.

"You're making a huge mistake," Blaine fumed. He walked out and slammed the door behind him.

Colin didn't say a word until the door clicked shut and they were alone. Then he turned so he was facing Andi. She was visibly shaking now, so he took her in his arms. "Hey, don't worry," he said. "He's gone."

She nodded against his chest. "I didn't think that would ever happen." She pulled back and looked him in the eye. "Blaine and I, we're over," she said. "After what he did, I could never..."

"The baby?"

Fresh tears sprang from her eyes. "I couldn't tell you. It was too hard." She swiped at her face with the back of her hand. "Besides, it's not like we're dating or anything." She tried to smile, but Colin could see the strain. "You don't need to be bothered with these things, I mean—"

"Andi," Colin cut her off. He cupped her face with his hands and stroked her cheek softly. "It's alright. We have time to learn about each other." He touched his lips to hers in a soft, sweet kiss. "And I want to know everything," he said when he pulled away.

"Everything?" Tears glistened in her eyes and on her cheeks.

"Absolutely everything," he said.

Her mouth turned up into a smile. "That might take a little while."

"Good," he said. "Because I plan on being around for a while." Colin leaned forward and kissed her again.

It was Andi who pulled away first. "Just to be fair," she said. "I have to tell you one more thing."

He nodded, waiting.

"I think I'm falling in love with you."

Colin cleared his throat and laughed. "Well, thank goodness," he said. "Because I know that I'm absolutely, crazy in love with you."

Colin kissed her again, this time leaving no room for questions. When the kiss ended, too soon for his liking, Andi was smiling. "So," she said. "How about that second date?"

If you enjoyed Unexpected Gifts...you'll love the continuation of Andi and Colin's story in the short story Unexpected Endings! I've included it as a special gift, just for you! Keep reading right after this.

But wait! Andi and Colin aren't the only ones who find love at Castle Mountain Lodge...

A woman looking for a fresh start...a single dad with his own heartache...and one little girl who just might be able to bring them both together.

See what happens in Hidden Gifts.

I've included a sneak peak of Hidden Gifts at the end of this book so you can check it out.

AND...don't forget to join my mailing list where you'll be the first to hear about new stories, sales and promotions and giveaways!

You can join me here —>

https://elenaaitken.com/newsletter/

# UNEXPECTED ENDINGS

Return to the beautiful, rustic and romantic Castle Mountain
Lodge and catch up with Andi and Colin who prove that
sometimes Unexpected Gifts have equally Unexpected Endings.

# 1

---

*A*ndi pulled her car into the circular drive and stopped for a minute to admire the majestic main building that was the heart of Castle Mountain Lodge. Ever since meeting and falling in love with Colin Hartford, just over a year ago, the mountain hideaway had taken on an even more magical quality if it was possible.

I've become such a sap, she thought with a laugh. It wasn't too long ago that same type of romantic sappiness used to make her nauseous. Things have changed.

She glanced at her watch. It was already after lunch. Andi knew she should've left earlier. Colin was probably already waiting for her and after so much time apart while Colin was travelling for work, they needed the time together to reconnect. The last few times they'd talked on the phone things had seemed so strained. Andi tried to shake the negative thoughts from her head and focus on the present. Now that they were at the Lodge, everything would get back to normal. What they had together was strong, they just needed to rediscover it. And the very same villa where they'd fallen in love, was just the place.

She put the car in gear and drove the rest of the way up the driveway, eager to get the weekend started.

Leaving the car and her bags with the valet, Andi tried to be relaxed as she walked through the sliding doors into the timber framed main lobby. But her veneer of calm shattered when a familiar voice rang across the room.

"Andi! Andi Williams is that you?"

Andi turned just in time to see Carmen running across the lobby. She opened her arms, just as her old friend crashed into her.

"It's good to see you too," Andi said. "I've never seen you so... so...enthusiastic."

Carmen pulled away and made a big show of straightening her clothes and smoothing her hair into her usual semblance of composure. "I missed you is all," Carmen said. "It's been way too long since you've been here. Don't you have some parties to plan up here or something?" She pulled her friend toward the reception desk.

Andi followed. "You know Party Hearty would love to come up and throw some big shindigs, but you're doing such a good job at it," she said. The comment got a smile out of Carmen and she went behind the desk to the computer and started taping on the keys.

"Well, you know you guys get all the big jobs. So, we'll see you at Christmas?"

"You know it," Andi said. "Now tell me, was Colin surprised to see that I booked *our* suite? When did he get here? I thought I would have heard from him by now." Andi pulled out her cell phone and stared at the black screen. "Well that would explain it," she said with a giggle. "I probably should have charged it." She looked up.

"I'm sorry, Andi," Carmen said. "Colin's not here yet. He phoned a few hours ago to leave a message. Apparently his flight was delayed. He won't be arriving until tomorrow."

Andi's stomach clenched and a familiar flicker of doubt settled in her heart. With effort, she kept the smile on her face and shrugged off the negative feelings. "I'm sure he tried to call to tell me." She waved her cell phone in the air. "I should probably get to the room to plug it in."

She waited, focusing on Carmen's tapping and typing while her friend completed the check in process. Andi tried not to be impatient, but she was done making small talk and just wanted to get to the room to plug in her phone and check her messages.

ANDI HANDED the bellboy a tip and tapped her toe waiting for him to leave. As soon as the door closed behind him, Andi unzipped her bag and dug around for the phone charger. She located it among the silky negligees she'd purchased just for the weekend. They really weren't Andi's style, but Colin had been in the Caribbean looking after business for almost a month and she was determined to make his homecoming as special as possible. Which was why it was extra disappointing that he hadn't arrived yet. It wasn't a great start to what was supposed to be a special weekend.

Leaving the wreckage of clothes behind her, Andi returned to the main room of the suite and plugged the phone into an outlet in the kitchen. It took a minute before there was enough power for the screen to display, but as soon as it did, she punched in the code for voicemail and listened as Colin's voice filled the room over her speakerphone.

"Hey, sweetie. You must have forgotten to charge your phone again." Andi smiled at how well he knew her. "I'm so sorry, Andi," Colin continued. "I know you have everything planned for this weekend but there was a big meeting and I missed my flight out of Antigua. I can't get another one until late." Andi dropped her head in her arms and tried not to let the disappointment take hold. "But I'll be on the overnight flight so I should be up at the Lodge around lunch time tomorrow." There was a pause, and then, "Oh, and Andi. I can't wait to see you. We really need to...well, we really need to talk."

Andi popped her head up and stared at her phone. *We really need to talk?* Wasn't he supposed to say, "I love you" or something? What the hell did that mean? She stared at the phone for another second more before pushing the end button and getting up.

Without Colin, the romantic weekend she'd carefully planned obviously couldn't take place. Andi resisted the urge to flop down on the couch and feel sorry for herself. Instead, she turned to the large picture window and gazed out at the mountains. She walked to the patio, slid open the door and stepped out onto the wooden deck, inhaling the crisp scent of pine and fresh air. She closed her eyes and focused on her breathing for a few breaths before reopening them and fixing her gaze on the rugged peaks. Soon, a familiar feeling of calm flowed through her. The afternoon sun warmed her, but there was no denying the chill in the air that meant summer was over. She wrapped her arms around her chest and tried not to think about Colin's message. It probably didn't mean anything, it was just a poor choice of words. Yes, Andi decided. A very poor choice.

"I'm so glad you're here," Carmen said.

Andi slid into the seat across from her. "How could I refuse?" She asked with a wry smile. "Especially when you showed up at my door and practically forced me out."

"Hey, I do what I have to do." Carmen winked and Andi had to laugh. "Oh, and my friend Lisa is going to meet us here too,"

Carmen continued as she poured Andi a glass of red. "She works in the Cub Club and I think you'll really like her."

"I'm sure I will." Carmen's good mood was starting to rub off. She took a sip of wine and decided to make the best out of her evening. After all, she was at the Lodge and it was on of her favorite places, how could it not be a good night?

"Hi, you must be Andi," a pretty blond said as she slid into her seat. "I'm Lisa. I hope it's okay to be crashing your little party tonight," she said.

Andi instantly warmed to her genuine smile. "Absolutely," she said. "The more the merrier for a girls' night, right?"

Carmen handed Lisa a drink and all three toasted. "To girls' night."

"And thank goodness for that," Lisa said, after she put her glass down. "I'm so done with men. It's a nice change to be surrounded by estrogen."

"Oh?" Andi raised her eyebrows but it was Carmen that explained.

"Lisa just broke up with her boyfriend," Carmen said.

"But I don't want to talk about it," Lisa said with a wave of her hand. "Carmen told me about how you met your boyfriend. It's so romantic." Carmen coughed and Lisa shot her a look. "What?" Lisa asked. "Just because I have crappy luck with men doesn't mean I don't still believe in romance." She turned back to Andi. "I do think it's romantic. But why isn't he here now?"

Without meaning to, Andi glanced down at her drink and swirled the wine in her glass. "Well, he's supposed to be here."

"Supposed to be?" Andi didn't miss the skepticism in Lisa's voice.

"He missed his flight, and—"

"Let me guess," Lisa interrupted. "It was an important meeting? He's on the next one out, right?"

"How did you know?"

Lisa shook her head and let out a bitter laugh. "You think I've never heard that line before?" She lifted her glass to her lips and took a drink before she said, "Men are all the same. First it's all missed flights, late nights and business meetings. And pretty soon it's 'we need to talk' and 'it's not you, it's me' and then," Lisa lifted her glass, "you're here, drinking with women."

A sick feeling rolled through Andi's stomach and for a moment she was afraid her dinner was going to make a reappearance. Hadn't that been what Colin's message said? That they needed to talk?

Carmen gave her a worried look and turned to glare at Lisa. "I thought you said you still believed in romance?" She asked her pointedly.

"I do," Lisa said, and took another sip of her drink. "But I'm also a realist and when a man starts showing up late and saying things like, 'we need to talk', there's only one thing that will come of it."

Andi looked down at the table and started fidgeting with the napkin, folding it into a tiny fan.

"That's not what's going on with Colin, Andi," Carmen said. "Seriously. He'd never do that to you, I've seen the way he looks at you."

Her friend's words were meant to be soothing, but all Andi could focus on was the fact that Carmen hadn't seen them together in months, hell, Andi herself hadn't seen Colin in almost a month. And hadn't that thought been tingling in the back of her mind for the last few weeks anyway? How could a relationship survive if Colin was always travelling? If they weren't together and weren't communicating, what chance did they have? Maybe Lisa was onto something. Something Andi herself hadn't wanted to admit. She looked up and gazed out the window at the mountains reflecting the setting sun. Perhaps their relationship had run it's course and the fairy tale was over?

$\mathcal{A}$ndi woke up the next morning with the sun shining through the gauzy curtains and the cool, mountain air floating through the window she'd left open. Not sure if it was the fresh air, or a good nights sleep, but Andi walked through the still empty suite with a much different resolve than she'd gone to bed with.

After returning from drinks with the girls, Andi felt more than ever that the romantic weekend she'd planned and her relationship were not headed in good direction. In fact, after listening to Lisa talk about the signs she'd ignored with her own boyfriend, Andi could have sworn she was talking about her and Colin. She'd returned to her suite drained and unable to do anything more than fall into a restless sleep.

But now, with the lonely night behind her, Andi made herself a cup of coffee and went to the picture window to stare out at the imposing mountains.

"You're being ridiculous," she said to her faint reflection in the window. "You know Colin loves you and as soon as he gets here, everything will be fine."

Andi took a sip of her coffee. Colin should be arriving right before lunchtime, which meant she had plenty of time to hit the trails around the lodge and get some exercise. She just needed to steer clear of Lisa and any more negative thoughts; at least until she had Colin in her arms and his lips on hers.

After a quick shower and grabbing a muffin from the Lodge bakery, Andi spent the rest of her morning wandering the many kilometres of pathways that circled through Castle Mountain Lodge's various buildings, and eventually wound past the pond where Colin had taken her ice skating for the first time, through the forest and along the cliff where she could gaze down the valley.

There were so many memories for them in every corner of the Lodge grounds. When she'd run away to spend Christmas alone in the mountains almost a year earlier, the last thing she'd expected was to fall in love. But she certainly had. Not only had Colin taught her how much joy there could be in the holiday season, but he'd also taught her that true love was possible.

Andi wrapped her arms around herself, shivering from the cold breeze coming off the mountains. She forced any lingering negativity out of her head. After all, this was their place. The place where their love had first bloomed and no doubt as soon as they were together again, their hearts would remember how they felt about each other.

She glanced at her watch. It was after noon which meant Colin should have arrived at least an hour earlier. She tried not to frown and let the doubt creep back in. But Andi had left a note in their suite so that in case he showed up while she was still out walking, Colin would know exactly where to find her. She quickened her step eager to get back and see him. But at the same time, something held her back. Shouldn't he have been just as excited to come and find her?

She'd almost convinced herself that Colin had been delayed again and that's why he hadn't come searching for her, when she slid her key into the door of their suite and opened it to find Colin sitting in the living room, intently staring at his lap top.

His head popped up as soon as he heard the door, and the smile that lit up his handsome features almost undid all the stress and worry she'd created in the short walk.

"Hey, sweetie." He jumped up from the couch and in two long strides crossed the room and pulled her into his arms. "Am I ever glad to see you."

Before she could formulate a reply, his arms were wrapped tightly around her holding her close while his lips became intimately reacquainted with hers. It felt like it had been forever since she'd tasted the familiar combination of coffee and mint on his breath, but her body remembered exactly how to respond to his persistent kiss. With a groan, Andi pressed herself closer to him, ready to see for herself exactly how much he missed her.

But instead of sweeping her up in his arms and carrying her straight into the bedroom where Andi hoped they would stay for the next forty eight hours, Colin pulled away breaking their connection and leaving Andi with all her insecurities rushing back.

"Hey," she said, trying to keep her voice light. "I thought maybe we could skip lunch and go..." when he sat in front of the computer again, she didn't bother finishing the thought.

As if she hadn't spoken, Colin immediately started staring at the screen and furiously typing once again.

Andi straightened up and crossed her arms. "So," she said. This time her voice had an edge. "What time did you get in?"

She wanted him to say he'd just arrived. She silently pleaded for him to tell her he'd barely had time to drop his bags off, but when he didn't even bother to turn towards her when he said,

"Actually got in about an hour ago." Her throat tightened and she had to turn towards the window to keep from crying.

It was a beautiful fall day outside but it felt like an arctic blast had blown into the suite and Andi had to hug herself and rub her arms a little bit to keep from shivering. She waited for Colin to say something. Anything that would put her fears about their relationship to rest. But when she turned to check on him again, he was still intent on his computer.

"Colin?"

He hesitated for a second before turning in her direction. His face was lined with worry, frustration and something else she couldn't place. If she couldn't still taste him on her lips she might have thought she'd imagined his warm greeting.

"Is everything okay?" she asked after a moment. "I mean, you look a little...I don't know, preoccupied."

And not with her, she thought.

"Andi," he started. "I'm sorry. I have to deal with this." He gestured to the computer.

She forced herself to smile. "Okay," she said. "How about I make you a cup of coffee and maybe we could try for a later lunch?"

The skin around Colin's eyes crinkled with his familiar smile. "That sounds good, sweetie. I really am sorry. I just can't—"

The sound of an email coming through, distracted him and Colin returned his attention to the computer. With a sigh, Andi retreated to the kitchen and prepared them each a cup of coffee.

She waited another twenty minutes while Colin continued to ignore her. Finally, Andi stood and asked, "Do you think you're ready for that lunch now? Or maybe, I don't know... something together?"

Colin tore his gaze away from the screen. "Andi, do you think you could maybe entertain yourself for a bit? I mean—"

"Entertain myself?" Andi managed to force the words out. "You think that's why I booked a romantic weekend away? So I could entertain myself?"

"It's just that—"

"I don't think I'm asking for too much. I was just hoping for..." she turned to the window again, determined not to cry. Lisa's words the night before ran through her head again. "You know what?" She crossed the room without looking back. "I don't need this. Enjoy your romantic time with your computer."

It wasn't the best approach and it was probably childish, but if Colin was going to choose his computer over spending time with her, especially after she'd gone to so much work planning the weekend, well, Andi didn't see how it mattered if she slammed the door and left. Which is exactly what she did.

Of course the first person Andi ran into when she stormed into the main building of the Lodge was Lisa. She tried to duck behind a large potted plant before Lisa saw her. Andi definitely wasn't in the mood to hear anymore about how her relationship was absolutely screwed, especially since she was pretty sure it was. But it was too late. Lisa saw her, waved and started walking in her direction.

"I'm glad I ran into you," Lisa said. "I wanted to apologize for last night. I shouldn't have gone off about men and—"

"It's no biggie," Andi said with a shrug.

"No, it is a biggie. Just because my ex was a total jerk about the way he broke it off with me, doesn't mean that all men are like that." Lisa stuck her hands in the pockets of her jeans. "I'm sure your boyfriend is thrilled to see you and rushed to make it here this morning, right?"

Andi tried not to let her emotions show on her face, but she didn't trust herself to talk. Instead she looked down at her shoes and offered Lisa a shrug.

"He got here okay, didn't he?" Lisa asked, concern lacing her voice.

Andi nodded.

"Where is he?" Andi could hear the hint of relief in the other woman's voice and it almost undid her. "Shouldn't you two be locked away in a bedroom somewhere?"

Andi finally looked up and everything must have shown in her face because Lisa immediately went back to looking worried. "What's wrong, Andi?"

"I...I don't think he wants to be here very badly. He's been working since he arrived, I feel like I'm just in the way and he told me to go entertain myself. I mean, really?"

Without asking, Lisa took Andi by the hand and led her to two overstuffed chairs by the windows. She sank into the soft cushions and took a minute to compose herself. Whatever it was that was happening with Colin, she refused to let herself cry in front of a woman who was still virtually a stranger.

To her credit, Lisa didn't rush Andi into saying more.

"I just thought it would be different is all," Andi said after a moment. "It's been hard being apart, but over the last few weeks he's been preoccupied, and distant." She looked up into Lisa's concerned face. "Maybe you were right? Maybe he is pulling away and he did say he needed to talk." Andi let her gaze drift over to the window and the wild ruggedness that was beyond. "He's probably going to break up with me."

"You don't know that."

But in that moment, Andi did know it. She nodded and didn't stop the tears that built in her eyes. "It's the only explanation."

"No," Lisa said. "I mean, it might be the case." Andi shot her head up and Lisa quickly backtracked. "What I mean is, men usually have a reason for acting strangely, so—"

Andi nodded and shook her head at the same time. "You're

right. There is a reason, and I think I'm pretty clear now on what it is." She studied the other woman for a moment and Andi could clearly see the understanding in Lisa's eyes. She was looking at a woman who was bitter and jaded about men, and for good reason. But she wasn't going to let that happen to her. She shook her head and stood up with new resolve. "But I'm not going to sit around just waiting for it to happen to me," she said. Andi swiped at her eyes and straightened her sweater.

"What do you mean?" Lisa stood with her and eyed her warily.

"I'm going to march back into that suite and demand an explanation." She choked over the words, but covered it with a small cough. "I won't let him do this to me. Not here."

Without waiting for Lisa to reply, and with determination she didn't quite feel, Andi left the Lodge and started the walk back to their suite where she was pretty sure she'd find Colin, the man who was supposed to be the love of her life, still on the computer.

Doubt pushed in and she slowed her pace, taking the time to watch the squirrels run back and forth in front of her across the gravel path. It was impossible to know if she was making the right choice. There was no doubt in her mind that she loved Colin more than anything else in the world. But what if love wasn't enough? Especially if he wasn't feeling the same way.

She reached the solid, wooden door of their suite and with her heart cracking, Andi slid her keycard in and pulled it open ready to end her relationship, and with it, kill a little part of herself. No, a large part.

But when she stepped into the suite, it was empty. On the table where Colin's laptop had been, was a note with a sunflower laid across it.

Andi froze, unable to cross the room and read the note that was without a doubt, the end to her relationship. She stared at it, willing it to disappear. Finally, after what felt like hours, she slowly moved towards the paper and picked it up. She held the flower in one hand while she read:

*We needed to talk. Please meet me at the pond.*
*~Colin*

he pond? He was really going to break up with her at their special place? How dare he do this to her! With anger flaring through her, Andi clutched the sunflower in her hand and all but ran to the pond in the woods behind the Lodge. She'd be damned if she would let him ruin her happy memories of a place that held so much love and hope for her.

She broke through the trees and entered the clearing in front of the pond. Colin must have heard her because he immediately turned around.

Andi's breath caught in her throat at the sight of him. She almost never saw him in anything other than faded jeans and a t-shirt but standing next to the cascading waterfall, on a large flat bolder that jutted over the water, he was dressed in what looked to be brand new jeans, and the black button-up shirt she'd bought him for his birthday. It wasn't his clothes, but his smile that was her undoing. As soon as he saw her, his grin stretched so wide, she could see the skin around his gorgeous green eyes crinkle up in that way she loved.

Nothing made sense. The sob in her chest struggled to

escape, and with difficulty she swallowed her confusion and walked toward him.

When she got close enough to touch him, she wrapped her fingers around the stem of the sunflower to keep from reaching out. Colin's face transformed once again, growing serious and he lowered his eyes.

She opened her mouth to say the speech she'd mentally prepared on her way, but the words didn't come out, and looking into his eyes, Andi couldn't remember a word of what she was going to say. Before she could think of anything to say, Colin dropped to one knee and grabbed her hands, squishing the flower between them.

It took her mind a minute to catch up to what he was saying.

"Andi I love you more than life itself and being apart from you for the last few weeks has been absolute—"

"Colin, I—"

"No," he said gently. "Please let me say what I need to." She nodded, unsure of what she would've said anyway. "From the moment I met you," he continued. "I knew there was something special about you. Even though you didn't know how to ice skate." His lips curled into a little smile before he continued. "The last few months have been amazing, I'm sure now that we were absolutely meant to be together. I can't ever imagine being apart from you the way I was these last few weeks."

Andi's thoughts swirled wildly as she tried to register every word he was saying. And when he pulled a ring box out of his pocket and showed her the square cut sapphire set with diamonds, she suddenly didn't trust her legs to support her.

"Andi," Colin said. "I want to be with you always and I hope to hell you feel the same. Will you marry me?"

Unable to form a proper response, Andi nodded and the tears that had been threatening all day spilled down her face. She hardly felt Colin slide the ring on her finger. But when he stood and pulled her into a tight embrace, her body responded with reflex and she wound her arms around his back, meeting his kiss with her own.

She let all her thoughts and worries from the day melt away and instead focused on the man in her arms. When they finally pulled apart, Colin took her hand and together they walked to a bench on the edge of the clearing that offered them slightly more privacy.

"Are you happy?" Colin asked her, tracing her jawline with his finger tips.

Andi nodded.

"I was worried you wouldn't say yes," he confessed. "You looked pretty angry when you got here."

Andi looked down at the sparkling ring on her hand. "Well, the weekend wasn't really going the way I'd planned."

Colin took her hand in his and brought it to his lips. "I know, sweetie. I felt like such an ass earlier, but I was so nervous that I didn't trust myself to be around you without ruining my surprise."

Andi's heart flipped. "You've been planning this for awhile?"

"For weeks," he said. "I realized that it's not going to work with me travelling down South all the time so I've been making the arrangements to bring on a manager for the Caribbean division. That's why I was late. I had to meet with the guy I hired and then when I got here, I was finalizing the paperwork."

"So, that's why you were so distant?" Andi swallowed hard, trying to hide the foolishness she felt.

Colin swept a stray piece of hair behind her ear and tilted her chin up so she was looking him in the eye. "Of course," he said and placed a gentle kiss on her lips. "You didn't think it was anything else did you?" There was a sparkle in his eyes that gave him away. Colin had a very good idea about how her imagination could run wild.

Andi laughed, mostly at herself. "Let's just say, I'll never again take advice from someone who's bitter towards men."

Colin reeled back in jest. "Ouch. Never a good idea," he said. "Well I'm glad you came to your senses."

"Me too," Andi said.

Colin released her hand and cupped her cheek, stroking her skin with his thumb. "Trust in us, Andi," he said, holding her gaze.

"I do," she whispered. "Always."

I hope you enjoyed this bonus short story! I absolutely believe the mountains are a magical place and they hold a very special place in my heart.

If you haven't already, make sure you check out he sneak peek of Hidden Gifts for more love at the Lodge! You can read the first chapter right after this...

Don't forget to join my mailing list where you'll be the first to hear about new stories, sales and promotions and giveaways! You can join me here —>
https://elenaaitken.com/newsletter/

# HIDDEN GIFTS

**Please enjoy an excerpt from the next in the Castle Mountain Lodge Series—Hidden Gifts**

Castle Mountain Lodge was just gearing up for the busy summer season with only a few people milling around the lobby. As far as Bo Clancy was concerned, it was perfect. The last thing he needed to worry about was an audience on top of everything else. He paced in front of fireplace and glanced around again for the staff manager. He'd been told that Carmen would be in the lobby, but so far he hadn't seen her. It figured that just when he needed to talk to her, she would be busy. It was a good thing they still had a few weeks before the summer season was in full swing which bought him a little more time to figure out what he was going to do.

Bo had been set up to have another successful summer as the lead outdoor guide at Castle Mountain. He'd been running the summer program at the Lodge for the past three years and it was the perfect job for someone like him. Someone who'd rather be outside than in and most importantly, didn't have any family ties that would keep him from leading the overnight excursions. They were the most lucrative trips because of the tips involved, usually from the women. He'd gained a bit of a reputation as a flatterer and as a result was often specially requested to lead ladies' groups. He never acted on his flirtations, at least not with the guests, but it didn't hurt as far as the income was concerned.

That was all going to change this year, unless he could figure things out. Bo looked at the couch, where Ella was sound asleep. Curled up with his big cable knit sweater as a blanket, she looked impossibly small. Her blond hair was fanned out over her tiny arm that was tucked under her head. Her blond eyelashes fluttered against her porcelain cheeks. Bo stopped pacing and stood transfixed by her every breath. It didn't matter how many times he looked at the birth certificate and read the letter, he still couldn't believe she was his. He bent to touch her, to push the stray hair off her cheek, but he pulled away at the last minute, a familiar voice intruding on the moment.

Bo straightened up to see Carmen, accompanied by two other women, walking across the room. They stopped by the grand piano and he watched for a minute as Carmen gestured around the grand foyer. She seemed familiar with the petite dark haired woman, maybe they were frequent guests? But no, the other woman, the taller one, clutched a red binder in her hands. The Castle Mountain Lodge Employee Manual. He had one just like it somewhere in his bags. Not that he'd ever looked at it.

Carmen had never been his biggest fan. Not since the first year they'd worked together and he'd slept with her roommate. It was years ago and he was fairly certain the roommate didn't remember it, but Carmen had been frosty to him ever since. When he'd discovered that she was now in charge of staff, he'd been dreading the conversation he needed to have because based on past history, she wasn't likely to help him out.

Bo took another look at Ella who was still sleeping on the couch. "No time like the present," he said aloud. He turned and crossed the room in three long strides. "Excuse me," he said, interrupting the women. "Carmen, I need to speak with you."

Carmen turned, a fake smile that didn't quite reach her eyes, pasted on her face. "Nice to see you, Bo. I'm just in the middle of something right now, maybe we can catch up later."

"It can't wait," he said. He flicked his glance to the other women and his gaze naturally landed on the taller of the two. She looked to be in her late twenties, which instantly intrigued him. Older than most of the women working at the Lodge and she was attractive, very attractive. But she definitely had the look of a city girl who wouldn't know the first thing about stepping out of the mall and onto the trail. Despite her slender waist and curves that begged to have his hands on them, city girls weren't his thing. Even if he was looking for a diversion, which he wasn't. "I am sorry to interrupt, darling," he spoke to the her and turned on the charm. "You probably have a lot of questions about the Lodge and the mountains, after all, they can be intimidating. And I'm sure we can do our best to answer those for you later." Without waiting for a response, he turned back to Carmen. "I do need to speak to you right now."

Carmen cleared her throat and stood tall. "Bo, this is Andi Williams and Morgan Pierce." She waved at the two women in turn. "Andi is a good friend of the Lodge and Morgan will be working with us this summer."

He spared a quick nod but kept his eyes on Carmen. "Hi," he said in the women's direction. "Carmen-"

"Oh, I'm sure a big important guy like yourself can answer all the questions for little ol' me," the voice interrupted him, and Bo turned back to the attractive woman who was batting her eyelashes in jest. "And maybe when you're finished," she drawled, "you could protect me from all the big bad bears in the scary dark woods?"

Amused, and more than a little intrigued, Bo tilted his head and examined the woman for a moment. She batted her lashes one more time before her eyes hardened and challenged him. He'd underestimated her.

Next to her, the other woman stifled a laugh which Bo ignored. "I certainly didn't mean to imply that you were incapable of taking care of yourself," he said, a sly grin on his face.

"Of course not."

The two faced off, neither willing to break the stare. For a moment Bo even forgot what he'd come to talk to Carmen about but before he had a chance to say anything further, Carmen reminded him of his purpose.

"Bo, if you could just give me five minutes to finish up-"

"No," the woman said. Damn, he wished he'd been paying attention when Carmen introduced them. "It seems that, Bo is it?" She waited for his nod before continuing, "It seems that Bo here has something very pressing to talk to you about. I'm sure Andi can help me get settled." She ran a hand through her hair, a nervous action that contrasted completely with her no nonsense attitude and Bo had to hide a smile.

Despite his vow to focus on Ella, he couldn't ignore the familiar tug low in his belly.

"You're sure, Morgan?" Carmen asked.

Morgan, Bo remembered. He made a mental note of the name, he wouldn't forget it again.

She smiled at Carmen, all the challenge and hardness that Morgan had shown him a moment ago was gone, replaced by a warmth that he suddenly wished was aimed in his direction. "It's no problem, really," she said. "Besides, Andi has been dying to show me some of her favorite spots."

"It's true," Andi said. "And it'll give me a chance to enjoy the Lodge in the spring. Don't worry, Carmen. We can see that you're busy."

"Thank you both for being so understanding," Carmen said, shooting a dirty look in Bo's direction. She handed Morgan a piece of paper. "This is your room assignment. Your roommate should be there soon, if she's not already. There's just one more thing that I need to discuss with you. There's been a little change in your job assignment, but...you know what? I'll find you later to talk it over. Is that okay?"

"Sure."

"It was a pleasure to meet you, Morgan," Bo said in his most charming voice. "I'm sure I'll be seeing you again."

"I guess we'll see," Morgan said. Her arms were crossed over her chest, but Bo noticed the spark in her eye when she spoke. Was it a challenge? She looked like she might say something else, but her friend took her arm and led her away. It was probably for the better. He needed to focus on Ella and a woman like that would only be an unwelcome distraction.

The moment they were out of ear shot, Carmen spun on her heel to face him. "Bo, what the hell is wrong with you?"

"It's good to see you too, Carmen." His forced smile faded. "Congrats on your promotion by the way."

"Stop it." Her mouth was a hard line. "I see you still think your charm and good looks can get you whatever you want. But as you already know, it doesn't work on me." She tightened her grip on her clipboard.

"You think I'm good looking?"

Contempt shot out of her eyes and he quickly readjusted his approach. Bo leaned his elbows on the shiny piano top. He was pretty sure that charm wouldn't be enough to smooth things over with her, clearly, he'd been right.

"I did get a promotion," she said, ignoring him, "thank you. And I have a lot to do, so what's so important?"

"You know I'm looking forward to another busy summer up here," he started. "I always accept this position over any others that are offered."

"And others are offered?" she asked with a wry smile.

"You know they are."

"Okay." Carmen crossed her arms over her clipboard. "I'll admit it. You're the best, but why do I feel like you need something? I can't give you a raise, Bo. You already get paid more-"

"I don't need a raise." He spoke quickly and glanced over his shoulder to the couch. "But I do need a favor." Bo turned back to Carmen who was frowning at him. "My circumstances have changed recently and I don't think staff housing is going to be acceptable."

"Pardon me?" Carmen swallowed a bitter laugh. "Shall we give you a suite then?"

"That would be great."

"I was kidding," Carmen said dryly, her laughter cut off.

Bo looked around the near empty lobby and made a decision. He couldn't hope to keep Ella a secret forever, and Carmen was his best hope, his only hope really, to make the situation more comfortable. "Okay," he said. "Come here." He grabbed Carmen's arm and led her to the couch where Ella was still asleep.

"Who's this?"

"My daughter." It was the first time he'd spoken the word aloud. It felt foreign, but not entirely unpleasant on his tongue.

Carmen's face clouded with confusion. "But she's at least-"

"Four. She's four."

"I had no idea..."

"Neither did I." Bo gestured to an empty sofa.

When they were settled where he could still keep an eye on Ella, Bo said, "You can see my predicament?"

"I can see it," she said. "But I don't understand it."

Bo sighed. There was no avoiding the truth. "Ella's mother just died. It was breast cancer and it apparently moved quite quickly."

"That's terrible," Carmen said."

"It is." Bo nodded. "I knew Tessa years ago when we were in College. I had no idea she was sick. Heck, I had no idea she was pregnant." His gaze drifted back to the sleeping child as he thought of Tessa and how hard it must have been for her to have a child on her own. They'd both been young and stupid. Obviously, too stupid.

"You mean, you didn't know?"

Bo shook his head.

"Then? How?"

"I got a call from social services a few days ago. They told me Tessa had died about a month ago and left a child behind. Like I said, I had no idea that she existed, but apparently Tessa had laid it out quite clearly in a letter that she wanted Ella to live with me, her father. It took them a while to find me, I was-"

"I don't understand."

"Oh, trust me, neither do I." Bo ran a hand through his hair and looked Carmen squarely in the eyes. "Look. I know this is unusual, but I really would appreciate some help here while I'm figuring things out. I mean, obviously she can't stay with me."

Carmen raised an eyebrow.

"No," Bo said. "She's not staying with me. Well, I mean, she is. At least for a little bit, but I'm going to do some searching into Tessa's family. There has to be a better place for her to live then-" Bo stopped talking abruptly. Why was he telling her all this? He looked at Ella's tiny body, her chest rising and falling with every soft breath. There was a pull in his chest but he ignored it and turned back to Carmen. "Anyway, I need a little help. Just until I can figure things out. Ella's going through a tough enough time. She doesn't need the drama of living in staff housing."

"You're right," Carmen said. "It's no place for a child. But there's really no where else."

It was a long shot, but he voiced his idea anyway. "I know you were kidding but, what about a suite?"

Carmen half coughed, half laughed and quickly covered her mouth in an effort to quiet herself. After a moment, she regained control and said to Bo, "A suite? Please tell me you're kidding."

Bo didn't answer. Instead he waited her out, his gaze fixed on Carmen's face.

"Bo?" Carmen blinked hard and wiped her eyes. "You know I can't give you a suite. What about the other staff? The guests? The cost?" She flipped open her clipboard and started looking through the pages. "There must be an empty room available in staff quarters..."

He still didn't say anything. Carmen looked up. "I can't give you a suite," she said again. "Really, you shouldn't even have a child here. This isn't a-"

"Look." His voice was low, barely constrained. "I don't need to hear how you think I should or should not have Ella here. The fact is, she is here. Now can you help me out or do I need to find a new job for the summer?"

Carmen tucked her clipboard under her crossed arms and matched Bo's glare. "You wouldn't leave."

"Try me."

Tension sparked around them as they continued their stare down. Bo hadn't planned on threatening her with quitting. The fact was, he couldn't afford to quit. He needed his situation at Castle Mountain to work out. But Carmen didn't know that. And he was counting on her not calling his bluff.

A tiny noise, almost a squeak, came from the couch. The sound broke Bo's heart, and the stand off with Carmen.

In two quick steps, he was kneeling on the floor next to Ella. Hair mussed from her nap, her brown eyes were still clouded with sleep, but were open wide taking in the big room. He reached out and tentatively tucked a stray hair behind her ear. He moved to hug her, or hold her hand or maybe just touch her again, but he pulled away. Bo'd never been comfortable around children, and that hadn't changed in the last few days. The little girl didn't seem to be any more comfortable with him either and she pulled her legs up to her chest and hugged herself into a ball.

"Did you have a good sleep?" he asked.

She nodded and jammed her thumb in her mouth.

"Soon we can get settled in our room and then you can have a real nap, okay?"

She nodded again.

Ella had said only a handful of words since he'd picked her up. And the social services woman said she would only speak to the foster mother she'd been placed with, but even then, she didn't say much. Not that Bo knew much about children, but he thought for four, she should be talking a lot more. Of course, maybe losing your mother and living with a foster family before being handed over to a total stranger was enough to make a little girl clam up.

"Are you hungry? Do you want a snack or something?"

Ella shook her head and turned to look out the window.

With a deep sigh, Bo pushed up on his thighs and stood. Carmen was looking at him in that way that women have, when they've been affected by a small child or a puppy. The way that meant she was going to help.

"So, I can have the suite," he said. It wasn't a question.

Carmen nodded. "I'll see what I can do. But it will only be

for a few weeks until the busy season starts. And I'm going to have to charge you something for it."

"Take it out of my cheque."

She nodded and her expression turned to a frown. "Bo?" Carmen grabbed his arm and led him a few steps away from Ella. "Have you thought about what you're going to do with her while you're working? I mean, surely you don't plan on taking her on hikes with you. She's so tiny."

"I was hoping she could go to the child care room."

"Castle Cub Club?"

Bo shrugged. "Is that what it's called?" He smiled to himself. He'd never given the Lodge's child care program any thought. He'd never had to. "It's cute," he said and then quickly added, "I told you. It's just for a little bit. I need to make some calls. I think she has some family down East."

Carmen raised an eyebrow in his direction. But when she turned to look at Ella, she smiled and nodded her head. "Fine," she said. "I'll clear it with the powers that be."

"Thank you." Bo breathed a deep sigh of relief.

"This isn't a permanent solution." Carmen's voice permeated his thoughts.

"Don't I know it," Bo said with a vague nod. He partially listened as Carmen continued to speak about getting a room key. But his focus had already shifted squarely back to the little girl sitting on the couch. She looked so lost, so scared and so alone. At least they had that in common.

**How will Bo cope with being a new single dad? And what does Morgan have to do with it?**
**Read the rest of Hidden Gifts NOW!**

**AND...don't forget to join my mailing list where you'll be the first to hear about new stories, sales and promotions and giveaways!**
**You can join me here —>**
https://elenaaitken.com/newsletter/

# ABOUT THE AUTHOR

Elena Aitken is a USA Today Bestselling Author of more than forty romance and women's fiction novels. Living a stone's throw from the Rocky Mountains with her teenager twins, their two cats and a brand new puppy, Elena escapes into the mountains whenever life allows. She can often be found with her toes in the lake and a glass of wine in her hand, dreaming up her next book and working on her own happily ever after with her mountain man.

*To learn more about Elena:*
www.elenaaitken.com
elena@elenaaitken.com

Made in the USA
Columbia, SC
19 November 2020